ROSAMUND

At thirty-nine, Sir Hugh Eavleigh is a confirmed bachelor. The discovery on the eve of his departure for the Earl of Carston's residence that this gentleman has a daughter of marriageable age fills him with foreboding. Too long has he been the target for match-making mothers. But the unconventional Rosamund and her wild twin, Harry, win the affection of the baronet. Soon he becomes embroiled in their madcap affairs — until he is in danger of being arrested for highway robbery!

Books by Julia Murray
in the Linford Romance Library:

MASTER OF HERRINGHAM
WED FOR A WAGER

JULIA MURRAY

ROSAMUND

Complete and Unabridged

LINFORD
Leicester

First published in Great Britain in 1978 by
Robert Hale Limited
London

First Linford Edition
published 1998
by arrangement with
Robert Hale Limited
London

British Library CIP Data

Murray, Julia
  Rosamund.—Large print ed.—
Linford romance library
1. Love stories
2. Large type books
I. Title
823.9'14 [F]

ISBN 0–7089–5314–X

Published by
F. A. Thorpe (Publishing) Ltd.
Anstey, Leicestershire

Set by Words & Graphics Ltd.
Anstey, Leicestershire
Printed and bound in Great Britain by
T. J. International Ltd., Padstow, Cornwall

This book is printed on acid-free paper

For
Gramps

1

It was late afternoon and Sir Hugh Eavleigh was rapidly becoming bored. The gentle rocking motion of his chaise as it proceeded on a leisurely course proved sleep inducing and Sir Hugh decided it was time he reached his destination. Leaning out of the window he tapped the coachman with the top of his cane and instructed him rather acidly to 'put 'em along'. Then he settled himself back in his corner and sighed deeply. He was beginning already to regret his decision. His acquaintance with the Earl of Carston was of the slightest, and had some other scheme offered itself he would almost certainly have refused the invitation. None had been forthcoming, however, and he had not felt he could reasonably refuse the civil invitation on a mere pretext. The Earl, although generally easy going, was not a man to offend, and Sir Hugh had resigned himself to a bored month. The discovery, however, immediately prior to his departure, that my lord was possessed of a daughter whom, apparently, he was anxious to marry off, had nearly caused the baronet to cancel his visit, and it had only been from a sense of duty that he had made the journey at all. For several years he had had the doubtful honour of being the most coveted prize on the marriage mart. Mothers with an eye to his fortune had used whatever ploys they could devise to attract his attention, but even in his younger days he had rarely given an aspiring matron cause even to *talk* of ordering wedding clothes. Now, at an age a very little short of forty, only the most optimistic young lady could fancy herself to have any chance of ensnaring this valuable prize. In fact Sir Hugh, at thirty-nine, was rapidly falling into middle-age, and was showing no signs of regretting it. He was, as it happened, resigned to his bachelorhood, and had been so for some years previously. There had been a time, indeed, when he had quite confidently expected the day to dawn when he would encounter a lady with whom he could bear to pass more than a few hours. That day had never come, and it was but rarely that Sir Hugh regretted its non-arrival. The thought that now, after several years of immunity, he might once more be subjected to the wiles and ploys of an aspiring maiden almost made him turn for home, and he beguiled several minutes in determining when he might reasonably take his leave.

In spite of his staid character Sir Hugh wore his years well. He had even been well-looking, tall, and raven-haired, with a physique many men would envy, and if his cheeks had sunk a little of late, well, there were some who would think it only an improvement. The slight flair for dandyism that had characterised the youthful Hugh had long since passed away, and his preference now was for sombre colours and shirt points many a young buck would descry as paltry. The opinions of others mattered little, however, and at this moment Sir Hugh was merely hoping that the Earl might serve a reasonable table.

In response to his demand for greater speed the coachman had whipped up his horses, and now Sir Hugh, ever an unwilling traveller, was suffering the consequences of his own impatience. The road from Andover was notoriously bad, full of ruts and pot-holes, and, since a generous rainfall had blessed the country of late the journey was more than usually muddy. While Sir Hugh suffered every jolt before it arrived he was totally unprepared for a sudden lurch that threw him onto the floor of the chaise and brought the vehicle to standstill. Justly incensed, Sir Hugh picked himself up from the floor and, irritably brushing his coat threw open the door and jumped down into the road. A surprise awaited him.

The reason for their sudden halt was immediately apparent. Two mounted ruffians, impressively masked, barred their way, and were levelling pistols at the coachman and groom in a sufficiently threatening manner. Thus confronted, Sir Hugh halted in the road, and a frown puckered his brow in annoyance.

'Whatever were you fools about' he demanded irately of his servants. 'What the devil do I pay you for?'

''Ave a 'eart, guvnor,' said the taller of the two highwaymen in an accent heavily Wiltshire. 'Fired over their 'eads, we did. Never 'ad a chance.'

The coachman, pleased to find himself so exonerated, breathed a sigh of relief, and nodded in agreement at his master.

Repressing a strong desire to box the fellow's ears Sir Hugh turned on the two ruffians and demanded somewhat tersely what they wanted.

The taller man laughed. 'Gawd

bless yer, guvnor, the readies and the gewgaws!'

Despite the thieves' cant Sir Hugh readily understood the request and sighed. As far as he could see there was no help for it. The second man, little more than a boy, it seemed, had already urged his mount forward, and was levelling his pistol in a highly dangerous manner at Sir Hugh's nose. ''And it over,' he growled in an odd, gruff voice, ''an look sharpish.'

Reluctantly Sir Hugh dug a hand in his pocket and pulled out a fat leather purse which was immediately grabbed and pocketed by the youth.

'Now the gewgaws.'

Sighing, Sir Hugh unclasped the gold watch his mother had thoughtfully had engraved for him, and, together with a large ruby ring, dropped it into the fellow's hand, noticing as he did so how exceptionally white and shapely that small hand was. Then the watch and ring disappeared and the youth backed his horse away.

'Gawd bless yer, guvnor,' said the taller fellow, grinning cheerfully and preparing to back away.

Not only the thieves, but Sir Hugh himself, were unprepared for what followed. The coachman gave a sudden shout, produced a battered pistol he had hitherto concealed, and fired it in the direction of the boy. The bullet flew harmlessly by, but the horse, startled by so much confusion, reared suddenly, throwing the lad to the ground, and causing the pistol he held to be flung into the bushes in the process. The coachman immediately followed up his action by jumping down from the box and descending on the fallen thief in a purposeful manner. The other fellow seemed undecided. For a moment it looked as though he would help his companion, then the thrown man, realising what he was at, made a rapid gesture with his hand and cried out in curiously high-pitched tones:

'Get away for the lord's sake! I'll be all right!'

The fellow hesitated a moment longer, and then, driving his spurs into the mare's sides, turned, and galloped off down the road. The groom seemed inclined to give chase but Sir Hugh, striding purposefully towards the fallen figure, signified him to stay.

'Leave him be,' he said shortly. 'This is the important one.'

The lad on the ground — for he was indeed no more — was lying quite calmly, staring up at his captors through the slits of his mask with large, apprehensive eyes.

'I suppose we had better hand him to the magistrate,' said Sir Hugh, eyeing the young offender meditatively. 'Give me the pistol, John, and get back on the box.'

'Begging your pardon, sir, but will you be all right alone with 'im in the carriage? That's a nasty one, that is.'

'Naturally I shall be all right. I shall shoot him if he moves.'

A flicker passed rapidly across the boy's face, and then he lay back impassively as the coachman surrendered the pistol to his master.

'Are you hurt?' Sir Hugh demanded curtly. The boy shook his head. 'Then get into the chaise. This is the end of the business for you.'

Silently the boy stood up, and walked with his head high to where the carriage door stood open. Having cast one apprehensive glance at the tall figure of Sir Hugh he clambered silently into the carriage and seated himself with his back to the horses. In a moment Sir Hugh, with the battered pistol carefully aimed, joined him, the carriage door was shut, and the vehicle jerked into motion once more.

'Well, lad,' said Sir Hugh, having contemplated the boy for a few seconds, 'I think we'll have your mask from your face.'

For a moment the boy hesitated, then with a swift movement undid the strings and let fall the mask that had covered almost his whole face.

'Good God!' said Sir Hugh blankly.

There was no mistaking. A pair of large, pansy-brown eyes regarded him impishly. The nose was short and straight, the lips curved upwards in the most tempting way imaginable, cherry red in a complexion of pink and white. As Sir Hugh stared in amazement the lips twitched slightly and the girl gave a little chuckle.

'Well,' she said, her accent thick, 'I never thought to be caught, you see, sir!' As Sir Hugh watched she put a hand to the close cap that so admirably concealed her hair and pulled it off sharply. The curls, long and brown, tumbled down about her shoulders, strangely incongruous against the rough breeches and jerkin she had donned.

'What the devil am I to do with you?' demanded Sir Hugh, considerably put out.

A dimple peeped in that fair cheek. 'Indeed, sir,' said the girl, 'you must do as you think, though I must say, I wish you might not give me to the magistrate! My Pa'll beat me if he knows!'

The idea of someone laying a finger on this exquisite creature had a strange effect on Sir Hugh. 'Your father?' he echoed, astounded. 'He surely would not dare!'

The girl nodded vigorously. 'That 'e will, sir, make no mistake! Allus angry 'e is. Even since I was born, 'e's bin angry. Angry then cos I wasn't a boy. 'E'll be angry now cos I can't do a man's work, after I told 'im so, an' all.'

'You mean he told you to go out and waylay carriages?'

'Yessir. I gotta earn my keep. Don't get fed if I don't bring home the ready.'

'The fellow deserves to be whipped!' exclaimed Sir Hugh in accents of horror. 'What does your mother think of it?'

The smooth brow clouded. 'Alas, sir, Ma's dead, two year since. Left me an' . . . an' Will alone with Pa.'

11

'Who's Will?'

The girl chuckled. 'You've seen 'im sir, this afternoon! Will's my brother! Looks after me, too, 'e does, right an' proper. Pa'll beat 'im, too, for not bringin' the earnin's home.'

'It seems as though it's your father who should be in prison,' opined Sir Hugh, consideringly.

'Oh no, sir, please sir, don't say nothin', I beg you! I know 'e's no good, an' all, but 'e's my Pa, an' I couldn't let 'im be took, not for me.'

'Well, what am I to do?' demanded Sir Hugh, his tone almost desperate.

The dimple peeped mischievously. 'Well, sir, if you want to 'elp, like, I'm hungry something *awful*!'

There was a short silence, then Sir Hugh gave a reluctant laugh. 'I suppose I should have guessed! Very well, but I should remind you that you have all my worldly goods in your jerkin pocket.'

For the first time the girl blushed. 'Oh!' she exclaimed, reddening guiltily. ''Ow *awful* o' me! 'Ere, sir.' Rummaging inside her buff jerkin the girl pulled out Sir Hugh's purse, and, after a moments hesitation, his watch and ring.

Sir Hugh received the purse, and the large ruby ring, but then said: 'Keep the watch, child. It might pacify your father.'

Of a sudden the girl looked uncomfortable. 'No sir, please keep it. I can't.'

'Of course you may. I would give you money, but I might need it myself. It is of no consequence. I can do without my watch, and would rather you did without your beating.'

The girl cast him a fleeting look, and fell silent, seemingly lost in thought. Sir Hugh, after regarding her consideringly for a moment, let down the window and leant out to hail the coachman. 'Pull up at the first inn you come to, John. At least I can give you a meal,' he said, drawing his head back inside.

A few minutes later they entered a village, and a marked slowing down of the carriage informed them that they were approaching an inn. Silently Sir Hugh descended to the road, and turned to help the girl out after him. She was strangely quiet, but smiled as she accepted his hand to the road.

The landlord of the Red Lion found himself torn. His feelings, when the knowledge, borne to him in a revered whisper by his good lady, that a member of the Quality was outside, conflicted sharply with his emotions on discovering that this apparently well-breeched individual had the intention of bespeaking a meal for some nameless urchin, and all this without the slightest explanation. He did not dare to refuse, but his comments, on returning to the kitchen, were less than complimentary to the baronet. Sir Hugh appeared unmoved. If he knew he was asking something out of the common way he gave no sign of it, and certainly his cool authority worked sufficiently on the landlord for him to produce a large cold collation within a very few minutes indeed.

As the splendour of the meal burst upon the girl the large brown eyes widened appreciatively. At Sir Hugh's invitation she seated herself, and began piling her plate with sundry delicacies. Sir Hugh was content to watch, and seated himself opposite her with a tankard of the landlord's best ale.

'Don't you think you should tell me your name?' he said presently, smiling at her enthusiasm.

'Rose,' she enunciated obscurely through a mouthful of roast beef. 'What's yours?'

'Eavleigh. Sir Hugh Eavleigh.' A second later he was on his feet, helpfully slapping the back of the girl, who had been seized by a sudden paroxysm of coughing. The fit subsided at last, however, and Rose was able to take a relieving sip of water.

'Thank you,' she managed at last, smiling up charmingly at the ever-helpful baronet.

Satisfied that no lasting damage had

been done, Sir Hugh sat down again and contemplated her from across the table.

'Tell me, Rose, just how many carriages have you and Will waylaid?'

Rose shrugged and licked her fingers. ''Undreds,' she said, carving herself a thick slice of ham. 'Bin doin' it f' years.'

Sir Hugh's brows rose. 'And how old are you now?'

The white brows puckered in an effort of concentration. 'I dunno. My Pa says I'm nineteen, but I seem to 'ave lived much longer 'n that.'

Sir Hugh smiled. 'And how old is Will?'

Again the shrug. 'Dunno. Older 'n me, though.'

Sir Hugh nodded thoughtfully. 'Does he always ride with you?'

'Oh yes! Will does all the firing, see, an' I collect the gewgaws.'

Sir Hugh found himself tempted to laugh, but sternly controlled himself. 'And has Will never been caught?'

The great eyes widened. 'No! Pa'd *skin* 'im!'

At this mention of the fearsome father Sir Hugh grew grave. 'What will happen to you because of this?'

'I dunno. I shall 'ave to go 'ome, o' course, cos Will'll worry 'bout me, but now I've got your watch p'raps 'e won't beat me so hard.'

'I hate to think of you going back there at all. Have you no one else?'

Rose shook her head. ''E'd only find me.' Licking her fingers carefully Rose scraped back the chair and stood up. 'I shall 'ave to go,' she said, 'or 'e'll 'ave my 'ide. Can I take my 'orse?'

'Naturally you may. It's outside. Are you sure there's nothing else I can do for you?'

'No. Thanks for the meal. I 'aven't eaten so well in ages.'

Somewhat reluctantly Sir Hugh got to his feet and accompanied the girl out to her horse. It grieved him to let her go back to such a welcome, but there seemed no help for it, and he watched silently as she mounted unaided onto the back of the mare. Safely in the saddle she smiled impishly down at him, a mischievous twinkle in her brown eyes, then the horse was kicked up, and she trotted from the yard.

2

Once away from the inn the girl kicked her mare into a canter. Several times she looked back, anxious to confirm that no pursuit was being made. Outside the village she reined in, and proceeded along the grass verge at a walk. It was a warm evening in early autumn but the nights were drawing in, and she wanted to be home before she was missed. About a mile out of the village she caught the sound of hooves, and, in a sudden panic, urged the mare to push through the hedge into the field. For an anxious moment she peered surreptitiously over the hedge, then gave a cry of relief as a familiar figure appeared.

'Harry!'

A tall young man, a black mask looped carelessly about his neck, reined in abruptly, and turned anxious eyes towards the hedge.

'Ros! For the lord's sake, Ros, are you all right? I've been worried almost mad about you!'

The girl laughed, and urged the horse back through the hedge. 'I'm sorry, Harry,' she said, all vestige of accent gone. 'It was so clumsy of me! But it was all right. I've so much to tell you!'

'Well, thank heaven's you're safe,' said the young man, wheeling his horse about. 'Lord knows what I would have told father when you didn't appear at dinner!'

'Oh, you'd have thought of something, Harry,' the girl said, seemingly unconcerned. 'After all, you always do.'

The young man gave a grin surprisingly like her own and brought his horse abreast of hers. 'It was a mistake, I suppose, to risk the daylight, but I had to see if it could be done!'

'You always were half-mad, Harry,' remarked his sister matter-of-factly.

The young man grinned again. 'And what of you, fair Rosamund? I sometimes think a devil lurks beneath those glorious curls!'

Rosamund took no offence, but merely chuckled softly.

'But do tell me, what happened on the chaise? How did you get away? I was bound for Upavon to break you out!'

'Oh Harry, you will never guess! He gave me a meal! Now don't look so incredulous, it's true, indeed it is! Poor man, he felt so sorry for me, and no wonder, with the tale I told him! But that's not the sum of it. Have you no idea who he was?'

Harry, who was scowling, shook his head.

'Only our dear Papa's revered guest. Sir Hugh himself!'

There was a pause, and then Harry laughed. 'Lud, but that's a rum thing! How much did we sting him for?'

After a moment's hesitation Rosamund replied: 'I don't know, I gave it back.'

'You what?' Harry sounded incredulous.

'I had to, Harry, he asked for it. Besides,' she added, with a little chuckle, 'he needed the money to pay for my meal!'

Harry smiled reluctantly, but seemed little appeased. 'The ring and watch too, I suppose.'

'Well, yes, but he was so affected by my tale of hard-ship that he gave me back the watch so that my 'Pa' wouldn't beat me so hard!'

Harry snorted and glanced at his twin with something like admiration. 'Well, it's not badly done, I suppose,' he conceded generously, 'though I wish to goodness I'd known you were safe! There I was, riding *ventre à terre* to rescue you from the hangman's noose only to find you've been dining with a baronet, as calm as you please, besides giving the fellow back his rolls of soft!'

'But Harry,' protested Rosamund, laughing, 'you didn't need it!'

Suddenly the young man grinned

and eyed his twin cheerfully. 'Too right, oh sister. But what will we do about this Eavleigh fellow? Will he be angry when he finds out?'

Rosamund frowned. 'I don't know. He might well resent me, but I don't think he'll hand us over.'

'He'd better not try,' exclaimed Harry, his brow darkening. 'But I could cope with that as long as he doesn't tell father!'

Rosamund maintained a silence for a few moments, and then said: 'I think I shall not come down to dinner tonight, Harry. The chances are he won't recognise you, and perhaps I'll have thought of something by morning.'

'Well, I only hope you do!'

★ ★ ★

Viscount Kearsley and Lady Rosamund Daviot were the children of the Earl of Carston, born within an hour of each other. They were ever wild, taking after their mother, who had bewitched the

Earl into marrying her when all agreed him to be a case-hardened bachelor. Always untameable, their mother's death some two years previously had severed what little control their father had had over them, and he, an easygoing man, had been content enough to let them be. They were a handsome pair, tall and slender, and, while they were not identical, there was a certain elusive similarity between them, in the line of nose and jaw, and in a certain twinkle that often lit the eyes of both.

None of his father's gentle nature seemed to have penetrated Harry. He had a love of life and a carelessness of danger, laughing at peril and encouraging it. He was quite untroubled by conscience, and while he made friends easily for his open, cheerful nature, his sister alone commanded his respect.

She was very like him. Constant companions, as children they had needed few other friends, for Rosamund was as ready as her brother for the most outrageous exploit. Only occasionally had she cast a dampener on her brother's schemes, and this not from any sense of personal danger. Never once had she agreed to the tormenting of their father, whom she loved in spite of Harry. Of late, too, she had noticed a certain reluctance in herself to join in some of Harry's wilder schemes, and she was beginning to wonder whether the time was approaching when they would begin to draw apart. She felt herself maturing faster than he, and knew that by twenty many girls were long since married.

She knew why Sir Hugh had been invited. A season in London had been ruled out of the question — it was too near her mother's death, and Lady Harriet Daviot, the only female connection suitable to launch a young lady into society was too old, and too infirm to oblige. The Earl, however, mindful of his paternal duties, had decided it was time his daughter made her own way, and had invited Sir

Hugh with the praiseworthy intention of ensnaring him as a son-in-law. Harry had been equally well aware of this plan, and the two of them had laughed about it, Rosamund bearing her proper share of teasing. But how Harry would react should such an event ever take place Rosamund could not conjecture.

Harry was not without his share of amorous intrigues. Rosamund had several times been called upon to assist in his love-life, helping to smuggle him out of the house, and excusing his frequent absences to their father. But the future for Harry was relatively unimportant. In ten years or so he would inherit, he would be an Earl, the family estate, Daviot, would be his, and he would have untold wealth to squander as he wished. He had no thought of marriage, and doubtless saw his life stretching away much as the past had been. But Rosamund had no desire to slide into middle-aged spinsterhood. Since a London season could not be contemplated for the moment she must make her own life, but so far her plans for this had only been the vaguest ones.

The threat of Sir Hugh Eavleigh had merely complicated matters. She knew perfectly well that her father would consider his duty done by her should Sir Hugh offer for her, but she had no intention of submitting to a whim. And now the affair on the road had made everything so much worse! Sir Hugh, if he did not turn them over, would doubtless leave in a fury, and her father would be more than ever determined to get her off his hands.

They had been back at Daviot barely ten minutes before the chaise conveying Sir Hugh rolled to the front door. Rosamund observed the arrival from the window of her chamber, and the sight of his tall, square figure confirmed her in her determination not to descend to dinner.

Sir Hugh's mood as he was bowed into the high entrance hall was deeply thoughtful. The little vagabond creature had affected him, and not only, he had to admit, because of her forlorn circumstances. In fact he regretted it much that he was unlikely to see her again. He wished he had been able to do more, but his ring was an heirloom, and he was, moreover, reluctant to help the villainous father and probably equally rascally Will. But the thought of Rose being beaten was almost unbearable, and he involuntarily shut his eyes as he thought of the belt being laid across that lily-white skin.

The Earl of Carston was there to receive him. He was a man of but average height, his dark hair shot with grey, with a long, sensitive face. The grey eyes were kind, but the chin, receding slightly, was indicative of his undemanding nature. He smiled now as his guest approached him, and held out a hand in greeting.

'Welcome, sir, welcome! How pleasant to see you at Daviot! I hope you had a tolerable journey. Holmes will show you to your chambers, then we will meet in the drawing-room. My son and daughter will be down directly. They are most anxious to meet you.'

Stifling a sigh, Sir Hugh allowed himself to be conducted up the sweeping oak stairway, and along thickly carpeted passages to a suite of rooms in the far wing of the house. His valet, having been sent ahead as was Sir Hugh's custom, was already awaiting his master's arrival, and Sir Hugh found himself with little to do but submit to having his boots pulled off and approve the servant's selection for the evening's dress. As the valet carefully brushed the discarded coat and bore it reverently to the closet Sir Hugh found himself strangely irritated by the leisurely attitude he had maintained for the past few years, and felt of a sudden an urge to be active, to descend to dinner without bothering whether his cravat was correctly tied or his severe black coat completely free of specks. It was a strange sensation, and one Sir Hugh was totally unable to account for.

He had resigned himself to the thought that, at thirty-nine, he had settled into a finicky middle-age, and to discover now a feeling that it did not matter if things were not just so was faintly disquieting.

Unaware of these thoughts his valet proceeded in his slow and stately way, causing the baronet greater irritation at every step. By the time everything was settled to the servant's satisfaction Sir Hugh's patience had almost expired, and it was with a sigh of relief that he escaped from the chamber and left the valet to potter on his own.

The Earl's mood, when Sir Hugh finally arrived in the drawing-room, was not quite as cordial as it had been. It was immediately apparent that something had annoyed him, and this was borne out by his saying, as he turned to greet his guest:

'It seems my daughter has taken it into her head to be indisposed. Why, just at this moment, I cannot conjecture. It is really most inconvenient. However,

I suppose we must just humour her on this occasion.' Obviously very put out the Earl crossed the thickly carpeted floor and gave the bell-rope an impatient tug. 'Not that Rosamund is generally subject to petty ailments. Not at all. We are all as a rule very hale. She is a strong girl, in spite of her appearance. I had hoped she would be down tonight so that you could meet her, but I daresay tomorrow will serve just as well.'

It was apparent to Sir Hugh that tomorrow would not serve just as well, as far as the Earl was concerned, and he found himself wondering just how many society hostesses would absent themselves on the first night of their guest's arrival. The Earl made an attempt to throw off his ill-humour saying as the servant opened the door: 'Is Harry down yet? We will dine as soon as he is ready.'

'If your daughter is truly indisposed I would not want to disturb her just for me,' said Sir Hugh, smiling very slightly.

'No, of course you would not. I daresay we shall do very well, just the gentlemen. Ah, Harry, come and meet our guest. Eavleigh, my son, Viscount Kearsley.'

Harry grinned cheerfully, and extended a hand to the older man. 'Call me Kearsley,' he said, grinning, 'everyone does.'

'I shall be honoured,' responded Sir Hugh, smiling at this carelessly open young man. Harry grinned back, and Sir Hugh suddenly found himself wondering where he had met this young man before. There was something elusively familiar about his face.

'I suppose there is no change in your sister?' inquired the Earl, not very hopefully.

'No, sir, I regret to say. Her maid told me just now that her head is so painful she had taken some laudanum and gone to bed.'

'Cursed nuisance,' muttered the Earl.

'However, I daresay we shall do very well on our own.'

★ ★ ★

For several hours Rosamund lay in silent contemplation of her problem. The watch he had given her weighed heavily on her conscience, and lay, snug beneath her pillow, burning a hole in her ear. She had long since determined to return it, but how this might be achieved without embarrassment or awkwardness she could not devise. In spite of her anxiety on the subject she could not help chuckling as she thought of how splendidly she had carried off her part and bam-boozled poor Sir Hugh. How he would react, however, on her unmasking was another matter, and her laughs subsided as she thought of the possible repercussions of their actions. It was not long, too, before the thought occurred to her that perhaps Sir Hugh might think it all a plot, a plan between her and Harry to make him look foolish. The idea was unwelcome, and if Sir Hugh knew just why he had been cajoled into visiting Daviot he would be even harder to placate. It was all very awkward, and Rosamund found herself wishing, for perhaps the first time, that Harry's inclination was not towards the most reckless and foolhardy of feats. Thus worrying her time away it seemed hardly credible that Sir Hugh was really coming up to bed so soon, and, she listened a moment to make sure, her brother also. Fumbling on the shelf beside her bed she discovered the tinder-box and with a little difficulty lit her candle. A glance at Sir Hugh's gold watch assured her that it was, in fact, past twelve, and she had been lying in her room for four hours or more. With this discovery her impetuous instincts returned, and she scrambled out of bed. By the inadequate light of the flickering candle she struggled into her clothes, the pair of Harry's old breeches she had worn earlier in the day. She glanced meditatively at her tumbled brown curls, and then discarded the idea of confining them once more beneath her tight brown skull-cap. Giving her hair a rebellious toss she caught up Sir Hugh's gold watch, and proceeded on tiptoe to the door of her room.

It had taken her some little time to dress, and consequently it was onto a darkened and silent passage that she opened the door. Leaving the candle behind her she stole out into the corridor, closing the door with practised stealth. Then, her hand on the wall beside her, she walked swiftly and silently along to the wing where Sir Hugh had been allotted his apartment.

In spite of the fact that she was certain Sir Hugh would, by this time, be aware of nothing, she hesitated for several minutes outside his door, straining her ears for the slightest sound. None was forthcoming, and, after scanning the darkened passage for the slightest glimmer of light she turned the carved handle softly and slid into the room.

Pressing herself against the wall Rosamund waited as her eyes accustomed themselves to the dim room. As was his custom Sir Hugh had thrown back the window curtains on retiring, and a soft silver glow illuminated a long rectangular section of deep, rich carpet, casting into faint relief the high square bed on which reposed Sir Hugh. The curtains about the bed were likewise drawn, and as Rosamund strained her ears she caught the steady up and down of Sir Hugh's breathing. There was no doubt that he was asleep, for the breathing was slow and regular, with an occasional soft snore as confirmation. Accordingly she eased herself away from the wall and crept across the thick pile to the prone figure on the bed. Casting one doubtful eye at Sir Hugh's face, which was turned in her direction, she produced the watch from her breeches pocket and deposited it on the bedside table. At once a hand shot from beneath the covers and caught her wrist in a painful grasp. Sir Hugh, tossing back the bedclothes, revealed himself in a long white nightshirt, his cap askew on his head.

'What the devil do you think you're playing at, you young rascal?'

The grip on her wrist tightened and Rosamund, giving a little gasp of pain, blurted out: 'Please, sir, I was only returning the watch!'

There was an exclamation. Sir Hugh, startled into dropping the girl's wrist, watched in amazement as she fled across the room, fumbled with the latch on the long window and disappeared. Coming to his senses Sir Hugh hastened across the room and arrived at the now open window in time to see the small figure scramble down the gnarled walnut tree that grew outside and run off across the lawn.

His brow puckering thoughtfully Sir Hugh closed the window and walked across the room towards the little table beside his bed. Even in the dimness he recognised it. It *was* his watch, so it must have been Rose. Yet he could not have been mistaken. In spite of the fact that she had departed somewhat hurriedly though his window, he knew perfectly well that she had entered through the door, that she had come from somewhere inside the house.

3

Panting slightly Rosamund gained the shelter of the trees and turned to look back at the dark outline of the house. There was no flicker from where she knew Sir Hugh's window must be, and she hoped fervently that he had dismissed the whole affair and returned to bed. She did not want him summoning the household and conducting a search of the grounds. As it was, she had to get back into the house undetected, but this was not a difficult operation. When she was fully satisfied that no alarm had been raised she crept from the cover of the trees and ran across the lawns in the direction of the South wing. All was darkness here too, but as she stood staring up at the lofty building she could easily distinguish in the glow of moonlight the dark rectangle that was Harry's window. A brief scrabble on the ground and a handful of small stones were sent up into the air to clatter against the glass and stonework and fall back, thudding on the ground. A brief pause, and then a glimmer of light appeared in the recesses of the room, the curtains were drawn back and Harry's face appeared at the window. Rosamund signalled rapidly, and with a curt nod Harry disappeared from view. At once Rosamund took to her heels again, running round the square house in the direction of the stables courtyard. She had a few minutes to wait by the low wooden door through which the Earl was accustomed to pass when going riding, and then a key scraped in the lock and Harry's head, his hair tousled and disturbed, was poked round the door. No word was exchanged, but Rosamund slipped inside, and Harry rapidly made fast the door behind her. Then they hurried silently along the narrow passage and up some winding backstairs to the second floor.

When they reached Harry's chamber Rosamund hesitated, and then followed him inside and shut the door.

'How the devil did you get outside?' demanded Harry crossly, hurriedly snuffing his flickering candle.

'Eavleigh saw me. He must have been awake, and I had to escape down the walnut tree.'

Harry shot her a quick look. 'Just what were you doing in Eavleigh's room?' he demanded, perching on one end of his rumpled bed.

'Putting the watch back.'

Harry rolled his eyes but said merely: 'Good thing you put on your breeches, or the fat would really be in the fire.'

'If it isn't already! I half expected him to wake Papa!'

'Lord, Ros, you're losing your touch! You were never wont to be so clumsy!'

'No! I shall have to face him tomorrow, but indeed, Harry, I could not have done it with the watch still under my pillow!'

For a moment Harry looked unconvinced, and then he nodded. 'Get to bed now, my Rosamund, or you will be unfit to be seen!'

Rosamund smiled, and let herself out. In a moment she had gained her chamber and in another had discarded her clothes and was curled up in bed.

It was some little time before Sir Hugh was likewise in repose. The fact that Rose had come from within the house for a while puzzled him greatly; she had known exactly where he could be found, too. When the truth finally flashed upon him he found the answer to several problems, and cursed his own gullibility. She was, of course, the missing daughter, Rosamund. It was so obvious now he thought of it. That was why the boy, Harry, had seemed so familiar. Not only did he bear an elusive resemblance to his urchin, but he was, of course, the ruffian who had waylaid him that very afternoon. The reckless daring of the attempt drew Sir Hugh's reluctant admiration; the pair were certainly not without pluck. In fact, there had been something endearing in Harry's careless good humour that evening. But it was a rum thing nevertheless. He must wait until morning to find out why they had chosen to waylay him, but it could not but occur to him that it was, perhaps, a plot to dissuade him from offering for Rosamund. This thought made him laugh. There was no denying it; they were an odiously likeable pair. The more he thought about it the more likely it seemed that it had been calculated in order to discourage his amorous advances. Sir Hugh was not a vain man, and it seemed highly likely that such a volatile young lady might not welcome the attentions of a man very nearly twice her age. It was a sobering reflection, but it sobered Sir Hugh not one jot. In fact, he thought the whole affair highly refreshing. That he should at last have lighted on someone who did not care a fig for his money seemed to him like a blessing from heaven, and Sir Hugh began to think he might enjoy himself at Daviot. It was on that reflection that sleep, which had been encroaching upon Sir Hugh for half an hour or more, finally took possession of him, and he drifted away into highly entertaining slumber.

In the morning Sir Hugh felt curiously elated, and the strange mood of carelessness that had so nearly over-taken him the previous evening was greatly in evidence. In fact the valet, Steering, felt quite alarmed when his usually finicky master told him for the lord's sake to hurry up and not keep fussing him as though he were some dashed dandy. As a result Sir Hugh descended to breakfast with a curiously rakish air, his white starched cravat tied in a careless manner of which Harry himself might have approved. There was no disguising the severe black coat, but he had selected a more jaunty waistcoat than usual and entered the breakfast room with quite a bounce to his usually ponderous step. He was, in fact, setting out to enjoy himself for the first time in years.

He found himself alone for the meal. So far, a desire to forsake his habit of rising betimes had not yet overtaken him, and after consuming his customary meal of ham and eggs he collected his gloves and cane and went out hatless for a stroll.

Rosamund left her room warily that morning. Harry had already been in to tell her that Sir Hugh was long since up and had gone out for his constitutional, but she was nevertheless cautious lest he should appear before she was ready for him. There was no alternative but to admit everything, and she was only slightly comforted by the fact that at least he now had his watch. She found Harry in the breakfast room rather impatiently awaiting her, having embarked quite half an hour earlier on his second breakfast.

'At last!' he exclaimed, carefully wiping his plate with a hunk of bread.

'Now we can find old Eavleigh!'

Silently Rosamund seated herself and thoughtfully spread butter on a piece of bread. 'Would you mind if I went on my own? Somehow I don't think your unabated cheerfulness would be quite the answer.'

Harry shrugged and absently cut the corner off a large ham. 'Do as you like. I daresay it's of no consequence. I might take out a gun. Harris says there's a heron down on the lake. I thought I might try for it.'

'I just feel it would be easier for me if you weren't there, that's all.'

'Going to try your charms on him, fair Ros? I would have thought him too old, but no matter.'

Rosamund looked up at that, but said merely: 'I doubt if it would have any effect. I just wanted to stop him telling Papa if I can.'

'I'm sure your intentions are praise-worthy, Ros, but what can the old gentleman do, after all? He can hardly turn over his only daughter and his son and heir. Besides, you know perfectly well he's got his eye on Eavleigh for you.'

Rosamund stifled a sigh. 'I only hope Sir Hugh doesn't know. It could be so awkward.'

Harry grinned. 'He'll believe we were trying to deflate his ardour, you think? Well, it wouldn't have been a bad idea. Pity I didn't think of it. Mind you, Ros, he's not a bad fellow really. A bit of a slow top, perhaps, but what does that matter?'

'A slow top?' echoed Rosamund, amazed. 'Harry, why do you think that?'

Her brother laughed. 'I know you're a great actress, Ros, but after all, you never quite captured that accent, did you? There must be precious little in his top-loft for him to have been so taken-in!'

'You're uncharitable, Harry,' said his sister shortly.

Harry grinned and attacked the ham again.

Rosamund had some business with the housekeeper that morning, but just over an hour later, dressed for some unknown reason in her most becoming muslin gown, sprigged yellow to show up her dark curls, Rosamund wandered outside in search of Sir Hugh. She knew the direction he had taken, and now that her resolution was made did not hesitate in the execution of it.

Sir Hugh, from a vantage point in the woods, saw her appear from the front of the house, and with a smile twitching on his lips set out to meet her. He had walked quite a distance and consequently it was a little while before the Lady Rosamund saw him bearing down on her. For a second her courage failed, for Sir Hugh, striding along at a great rate, looked anything but the doddering gallant Harry had made him out to be. Then he had reached her, and to her utter astonishment and perplexity raised her hand to his lips and said with a twinkle in his eye: 'Lady Rosamund! How delightful to see you so recovered!'

For a moment Rosamund thought his senses had deserted him, and then with a start realised that not only was the mystery no mystery at all, but that Sir Hugh was apparently treating the whole affair as one great joke.

'Sir Hugh,' she began, 'I really owe you the most enormous apology — '

'Enormous?' he echoed, his brown eyes laughing at her. 'Now why enormous? Ah well, 'tis no matter. I, on the other hand, should pay you quite stupendous congratulations for having me so completely duped! I own, if I had not seen you enter my room last night by the door I would never have cracked your secret!'

'Really, Sir Hugh,' said Rosamund, flushing, 'I am most dreadfully sorry! I know exactly how it must seem to you, but please believe me when I say it was all an accident that we held you up yesterday!'

Sir Hugh's eyes widened slightly. 'Indeed! It did not seem wholly accidental to me! In fact, you and your brother seemed quite wholly determined!'

'Well of course we meant to hold up your chaise, but we did not realise it was *your* chaise!'

'No wonder you choked over that beef,' remarked Sir Hugh mildly, casting her a fleeting look out of the corner of his eye.

Rosamund saw the look and laughed. 'You aren't angry, are you! I'm so glad! We really rather expected you to lay an information, you know.'

'Which was hardly more than you deserved, nevertheless. Whatever possessed your brother to expose you to such a thing?'

They had turned by now and were wandering round the Park in the direction of the shrubbery but at this point Rosamund hesitated and glanced up at her companion. 'Harry wanted to see if it was feasible to rob by daylight. Fortunately I think his curiosity is now satisfied and he won't be tempted to try it again.'

Sir Hugh cast her a rather searching look. 'Do I gather he makes a habit of it?'

'Well, it wasn't the first time, certainly. Generally he doesn't run such risks, but he gets, well, freaks sometimes and there's nothing I can do to dissuade him.'

'And these evening jaunts of his, do you go too?'

'Well, sir, I could hardly let him do it quite unaided, could I? After all, if something happened to him no one would know where he was.'

'Good God!' said Sir Hugh blankly.

Rosamund's lips twitched as she looked up at him. 'It does not sound as though you approve, Sir Hugh,' remarked lightly.

'It does occur to me to wonder how he uses the money, certainly,' the baronet responded, somewhat grimly.

'Oh, as a rule he gives it away, he's very generous, you know, but occasionally something takes his fancy and he keeps it. Have you seen his snuff box?'

'That Sèvres piece?'

'He took it from Lord Wyton about six months ago. I keep telling him it's too easily recognisable but he will keep using it. It gives him a thrill, you know, to be walking always on the edge of a precipice.'

Sir Hugh rolled his eyes heavenwards but said simply: 'And what of the Earl? Does he permit all this?'

'He doesn't know, and I must beg you not to tell him. It could do no good at all.'

'So, you have some conscience, then?'

Rosamund blushed at the unexpected sting in the baronet's remark, and replied: 'Indeed, sir, it is how we are! I must ask you not to concern yourself with us. We were made to be wild.'

'Wild, perhaps, but lawbreakers? I suppose you realise this could end at the gallows for you both?'

Rosamund smiled then. 'I do believe, sir, it would give Harry pleasure to have the opposition of the Authorities. I doubt if there is a prison that could hold him.'

'That may be, but I must hope for your sake it will never come to that.'

'Sir, you do not understand us.'

'Harry no, though I must confess I found him an engaging enough rascal last evening, but I believe, if I may say so, that I am in a fair way to understanding you, Lady Rosamund.'

She gave a startled laugh. 'Indeed, sir, am I so easy to read?'

'I believe so, yes.'

'Well, upon my word, Sir Hugh, I am glad I knew nothing of this before or it would severely have damaged my self esteem!' The words were light and Sir Hugh smiled down at her with something very like paternal fondness. Rosamund, recognising this, was unexpectedly comforted and returned the smile. 'I do hope, Sir Hugh, that you will not curtail your visit because of this affair. I am sure my father would be distressed, as indeed we all would be.'

'There speaks the perfect hostess,' said Sir Hugh approvingly. 'As a matter of fact, Lady Rosamund, I have not the slightest intention of curtailing my visit, provided, however, that you do not again subject me to the rigours of your brother's imagination!'

Sir Hugh parted from Lady Rosamund in a mood of mild satisfaction. He felt sure the lady had no intention of encouraging his advances, and he viewed this as blessed release. In fact, he felt he might rather enjoy himself at Daviot.

Rosamund too felt relieved. She made her way quickly back to the house with the intention of informing her brother that all was now well.

She could not find him. A rapid search of the parlour and the breakfast room informed her that he had probably left the house, which opinion was confirmed a few minutes later by

Holmes, the butler, who informed her that he had last observed the Viscount headed for the west wing. Since this housed both the Armoury and the gun room Rosamund hurried there at once, remembering that Harry had said he might try for the heron that had been stealing the fish in the lake. No gun was missing, however, and although the long gallery was empty she could tell that two foils were missing from the cases on the walls. The double doors to the park stood open, so Rosamund at once hurried out and began scouring the nearby grounds for any sign of her brother. She found him in the woods. Holding up the flounced skirt of her best muslin to prevent it being soiled she peered cautiously among the tree trunks and was startled by a sudden shout.

'Ha!' came a voice in a rich west-country burr. 'Now I've got you, my pretty! Come back with old one-eyed Jake!' Harry, materialising from behind a tree, balanced a sword in each hand

and regarded her roguishly, one eye closed in an outrageous wink.

'Oh Harry, do stop fooling! I came to tell you Sir Hugh is not a bit angry with us.'

'Well, that's a relief, anyway,' said the Viscount, abruptly dropping both accent and foils. 'Go and change and I'll give you a duel!'

Rosamund hesitated, and then, her lips twitching as she thought of what Sir Hugh would say, she nodded briskly, turned, and hurried back to the house.

A few yards away was an unsuspecting Sir Hugh, absently swinging his cane as he weaved his way through the trees. He too was startled by a shout, but this time it was: 'Have at you, sir! Defend your honour and your life!'

Mildly surprised, Sir Hugh glanced round and found himself facing the point of a buttoned foil while a similar weapon quivered invitingly at his feet, the point embedded on the soft earth. Harry, one hand on his hip, performed a mock salute, and then, before Sir Hugh was aware, lunged forcibly at a point somewhere above Sir Hugh's left shoulder. The baronet gave a gasp, then a chuckle, and, dodging the Viscount's second thrust, hurriedly divested himself of his coat. Grasping up the proffered foil he checked swiftly that the button was not dislodged, and rapidly parried the young man's thrust.

'Ha!' exclaimed the Viscount in tones of unholy glee. 'Well parried, sir, but not, I think, well enough!' He lunged again, and Sir Hugh found his attention fairly caught.

A few minutes later Rosamund, shamelessly attired in shirt and breeches, was diverted to discover her brother and their guest apparently locked in deadly combat. She watched, amused for some little time, it gradually becoming apparent that however skilful a fencer Sir Hugh might be he was certainly in need of practice. Harry was gradually bearing down on his opponent, his foil swift and sure, while Sir Hugh only just managed to deflect the continual thrusts and lunges of the younger man. Then, as Harry sought to make an end Rosamund gave a sudden shout.

'Harry, the button!'

The Viscount's naked foil was aimed high at a point approximately over Sir Hugh's heart, but on his sister's cry he jerked his hand away, ripping open Sir Hugh's shirt across the chest and releasing a long thin dribble of blood. Aghast, he let the sword fall from his grasp and strode across to where Sir Hugh, a little pale but apparently not seriously hurt, was regarding him with a quizzical eye.

'My dear Kearsley,' said Sir Hugh, amusement in his voice. 'I hope you do not mean to make a habit of this! First my money, now my life!'

Harry gave a short laugh. 'Are you all right, Sir Hugh? Upon my word I'm sorry! I can't imagine how the button came to be off!'

'You checked it, I suppose,' his sister inquired dryly.

'Of course I did,' retorted Harry. 'It was just damned bad luck!'

Rosamund gave a wry smile. 'Bad indeed had I not been here.'

Harry looked struck.

'Well, there's no harm done, anyway,' said Sir Hugh, one hand pressed to his chest. 'If you will pardon me I shall change my shirt and remove the evidence of your — er — foul play!'

'Will you be all right, Sir Hugh?' Rosamund inquired solicitously. 'Shall I find you a dressing?'

'My dear Rose, it is hardly more than a scratch!' So saying, he executed a mock bow, and, with one hand still clasped to his chest, he caught up his discarded coat and strode off in the direction of the house.

'Well, at least he takes his injuries like a man,' said Harry, stooping to pick up the dropped foils. 'Not that he didn't have every right to be angry! I must say, Ros, he doesn't seem like he's reported, an ageing and frumpy gallant!'

'Frumpy!' exclaimed Rosamund in horrified accents. 'Why, Harry, that you should even think of such an epithet after the way he's behaved towards us!'

Harry's brown eyes twinkled mischievously. 'Well, at least you shan't have to worry about advances from him! He gives every indication of regarding himself as some sort of father figure. Rose, indeed!'

4

It was not long before Sir Hugh discovered that his stay at Daviot was having the strangest effect on him. His valet, Steering, was distressed to observe that, far from abating, the odd humour that had lately overtaken his master was as much in evidence as ever. In fact Steering was sorely taxed to discover any item of his master's wardrobe that was suited to this sudden and mysterious change of taste. It was some years since Sir Hugh had worn anything but the most sombre of colours, and to have the gentleman suddenly bewailing his lack of an olive superfine could only be described as alarming. Nor was this strange phenomenon limited to Sir Hugh's dress. The unfortunate Steering, entering his master's chamber punctually one morning at eight o'clock complete with the luke-warm chocolate Sir Hugh invariably drank was not a little disquieted on being told somewhat sharply to remove himself forthwith and not to present himself until a more civilised hour. Poor Steering felt quite confounded, and seriously toyed with the idea of summoning a physician in case Sir Hugh, for once, had taken a fever.

In other parts of the house, however, Sir Hugh's oddities went unnoticed. The Earl declared himself very well satisfied with his guest, and was pleased to discover that the reports he had received of Sir Hugh being a devilish high stickler were apparently quite unfounded. Harry, too, was rapidly revising his opinion, and was even heard by his sister to call him 'a very good sort of fellow', praise of no short order. Rosamund herself was unable to decide about the gentleman. In fact, she found him something of an enigma. Why he should concern himself with them was beyond her understanding, and although she was glad he and Harry seemed to have taken to each other she was quite at a loss to account for the quirk of fate that had drawn these two unlikely gentlemen into such good relations. For good they seemed, indeed, to be. After the near disaster in the wood the two had several times taken out the foils, practising their paces both in the grounds and in the long fencing gallery. Harry was ever the better swordsman, possessed of a lightning wrist and flexible arm, but Sir Hugh, once he had dusted away the cobwebs of several years' inactivity proved himself to be no mean contender. He was more heavily built than Harry and stood ever at a disadvantage, but once, when Harry's guard was incautious, Sir Hugh broke through and his buttoned tip came to rest lightly on the Viscount's shirt front. Harry had laughed and performed a mock salute, and Rosamund, who was watching, was relieved to discover that they were to be spared the usual run of anger and excuses that would generally accompany such a defeat. She found herself feeling very much in charity with Sir Hugh and began to hope that, with such an example, Harry might not persist in some of his more reckless pursuits.

So far these showed no signs of abating. Twice since Sir Hugh's arrival Rosamund had been called upon to excuse her brother's absence, once when he tried his hand at holding up the night Mail — an exploit that failed miserably and nearly resulted in Harry's capture by some conscientious outriders — and once to visit the latest object of his attentions. On neither of these occasions had his sister accompanied him, although she had been sorely tempted to assist him on the Mail robbery, chiefly out of fear for his safety. She had tried in vain to dissuade him from such a reckless attempt, but when, as a last resort she had announced her intention of going also Harry had for once come down with a very firm rejection of this idea. Rosamund was somewhat at a loss to account for this sudden change of attitude, and wondered whether it was because of her bad handling of the affair with Sir Hugh. In this, however, she was mistaken. It had recently been borne in upon Harry that Rosamund, by posing as a boy, was running a far greater risk than himself, and that he was not acting responsibly in encouraging her company. He had no intention of giving up his present mode of life; indeed, it was the only excitement he had, and until the Earl would countenance a London visit for him and Rosamund it must suffice. Not that he was dissatisfied with his lot. Indeed, he rather felt he was of the type to enjoy himself in a prison. There was the feeling in his mind, too, that while Sir Hugh was about it might be better if Rosamund took no further part in his exploits than she need. He counted on her to excuse him to their father when he was missing, but she made no attempt to cover for him when he was absent two days at a prize fight near Salisbury. She could not approve such things, and did her best on his return to quell his enthusiasm. It was a vain attempt, however, and for several days after the company was regaled with bloody tales. Although such expressions as *wistycastors* and *drawing his cork* might be beyond her, she could object forcibly to a description of just how the unfortunate loser had met his defeat.

When Sir Hugh had been at Daviot a week a party of guests arrived from various parts of the country. The Earl had been hopeful that by the time these persons arrived he would have something of a definite nature to announce about Lady Rosamund and Sir Hugh, but it was apparent that although each seemed vastly taken with the other — he had noticed this almost from the first — Sir Hugh had no intention of rushing his fences and coming early to the point. But then the Earl was a reasonable man and had long since decided that should Sir Hugh, big fish though he was, prove unacceptable to his daughter, he was not above offering her her choice. Two gentlemen were expected, a certain Mr. Garvise, who was possessed of a reasonable estate and fortune, and the youthful Mr. Gerard Culcheth. It had taken a little effort on the part of the Earl to invite the latter, who, although pretty plump in the pocket, was possessed of a mother who invariably travelled with him. She was an overbearing woman, and much though he would like to welcome the young Mr. Culcheth into his family the prospect of her ladyship very nearly dissuaded him, and it was only the thought of his father's fortune that had finally tipped the balance in his favour. Garvise was always a welcome guest. Unquestionably the gentleman, he was possessed of a comfortable fortune which, although not to be compared with that of Eavleigh or Culcheth, was sufficient to make the

Earl consider any proposal of his with favour.

The news that Garvise was shortly to be joining them greatly pleased Sir Hugh. Jeremy Garvise was a friend of long standing, and although the baronet was enjoying his days at Daviot very well Garvise would be a welcome addition.

The discovery that more guests were expected depressed Rosamund. It seemed as though her father were indeed determined to have her married and away, and the arrival of two more prospective suitors made her rejection of them even harder to contemplate. So far her father had said nothing to her about Sir Hugh, but it was plain that he was watching their apparently increasing friendship with great satisfaction. She was unacquainted with either of the gentlemen, but she held out little hope that her dream knight might just happen to be among this random selection of gallants.

Upon Harry the additions had no

effect at all, and, beyond teasing his sister on the subject, he gave the matter very little thought.

Sir Hugh was on a promontory behind the house when the first of the parties arrived. He had been lent a large chestnut by his host, and had already got into the habit of daily rides. Now, from his position above the house he had a clear view of the main avenue, and contemplated the sight of a light travelling carriage bowling along towards the house. His eyesight had ever been good, and from the small amount of baggage he could distinguish on the carriage roof decided it was his old friend Garvise and not the Culcheths. Accordingly he kicked up his horse and proceeded down the hill in a leisurely manner, arriving in the stables courtyard just as Mr. Garvise's team was being led away to water. Striding into the entrance hall he encountered Rosamund, who informed him that she had just now returned from showing Mr. Garvise to his chamber, a room next to Sir Hugh's own, in the East wing. The baronet therefore mounted the stairs two at a time and arrived at his friend's door in a mood of pleasurable anticipation.

Jeremy Garvise was a sensible man, younger than Eavleigh by some four years. He was of medium height, with a strong, yet sensitive face. The nose was hooked slightly, the mouth firm, the brown eyes alive and humorous. At thirty-five he considered himself, as did many, at the prime of his life, and wore his brown hair modishly cut *à la Brutus*, a style made fashionable by Mr. Brummell. He had a certain flair in dressing, and never failed to pass joking comments on his friend's sombre attitudes and dress. He was a general favourite, with the gentlemen as well as the ladies, for he had an easy address and resources sufficient to make him a burden on no one.

Sir Hugh found him now in his shirt sleeves, reclining full length upon the

70

enormous bed while his valet, a thin young man with an enthusiastic crop of sandy hair, tugged valiantly at one recalcitrant and highly polished boot. Sir Hugh had entered hard upon his knock, and Garvise, cocking one eye in the direction of the door, was surprised and delighted to discover the man he had thought of, until that moment, as some fifty miles distant, at his estate, in Gloucestershire.

'For the lord's sake, Hugh!' he exclaimed, sitting up so suddenly that the boot jerked off in the valet's hands, causing this unfortunate worthy to stagger back several paces. 'Whatever are you doing here, Hugh? I had no idea! Carston said nothing!'

Sir Hugh shrugged and smiled. 'No reason to tell you really, Jerry. I very nearly didn't come, not that I'm not enjoying it now, of course.'

Jeremy Garvise gave his friend a hard stare. There had been a most unexpected twinkle in his usually staid friend's eye. 'What are you about, you

71

old dog? The young lady taken your fancy?'

Sir Hugh laughed and reddened slightly. 'Devil a bit! Not that she's not a pretty piece, but I'm far too old for that sort of flummery.'

'So I would have said,' agreed Garvise, continuing to eye his friend thoughtfully. He gave a sudden exclamation. 'I know what it is about you, Hugh! I've been sitting here trying to decide what's different about you, and now I've got it! It's that cravat you're wearing! Wherever did you dig it up? It looks as though the dog's been chewing it!'

Sir Hugh smiled unperturbed, and dropped into the one chair that was not covered over with various items of Mr. Garvise's wardrobe.

'Affecting a new look, are you, Hugh? Well, not above time, I must say. Mind you, if that's what's in the wind, you couldn't do much better than to change that riding jacket for something more up to snuff. However, one can't expect miracles.' Garvise swung his feet to the floor and contemplated his friend once more. 'Know what's in the wind, Hugh? Not like Carston to extend invitations of a sudden, is it?'

'It's the daughter,' Sir Hugh replied, somewhat shortly. 'It seems he's taken some idea of marrying her off, why, I have not yet determined. Culcheth's invited too, you know.'

Garvise cursed softly, and dropped back onto the bed again. 'That woman too if I know anything.'

Sir Hugh grimaced, and stretched his long legs before him. 'With luck they'll concentrate on the Lady Rosamund, poor child. Culcheth's hardly the man for her, in spite of all the blunt.'

Garvise gave his friend another of his penetrating looks. 'What's she like, Hugh?'

Sir Hugh glanced up and chuckled. 'Well, I suppose I can trust you, Jerry. There's a brother, a twin, called Harry, and a wilder, more unruly cub I have yet to come across. You will not believe, my friend, that I first encountered this pair on the road, where they were disguised as ruffians and attempting to waylay my coach. They would have succeeded too, had not the coachman fired and scared the girl's horse. I thought she was a boy, and had the surprise of a lifetime when I got her in the chaise.' He chuckled softly at the memory.

'Good Lord!' Garvise exclaimed, sitting up again. 'What the devil did you do with her?'

'Well, she fooled me with a story of a tyrant father sending her out to earn her bread, and such a tale I never heard. Beatings with the buckle of his belt, no less. Mind you, she was dashed convincing. She had the most rustic accent you can imagine.'

Garvise laughed. 'When did you find out who she was?'

'That night. I was fool enough to feed her, mind you, and give her my watch to placate the father. The Lady Rosamund had a headache and missed dinner, and that night the little Rose brought the watch to my room. Only I was too quick, and saw her. There was little doubt after that.'

'Good Lord!' said Garvise again, regarding his friend with amusement. 'Did you tell the father?'

'I hadn't the heart, Jerry, indeed I hadn't! Mind you, the boy's a real rascal. He goes about waylaying vehicles for fun, and even carries Wyton's snuff box, as calm as you please.'

Garvise stared, and then gave a reluctant laugh. 'He sounds the very devil! But tell me, Hugh, what's he about letting the girl take part? Seems to me he needs a lesson.'

'It's her own choice, Jerry. She's as wild as he is, if not as careless. They're very close.'

'Well,' said Garvise, standing up and taking the fresh cravat from his valet's fingers, 'it seems we are in for a happy time! Perhaps the young Harry will even outweigh the terrors of the Culcheths!'

A few miles away a carriage was pursuing its stately way towards Daviot. The roof was impressively laden, and a few hundred yards behind a second, slightly less elegant vehicle was conveying the maids and manservants Lady Culcheth considered indispensable for a sojourn in the country. The first carriage contained but two persons. Of these the most noticeable was her ladyship, a tall bony woman of middle age with a strong hooked nose and a very determined jaw. The eyes, which were unusually bright, were set a little close together, and of such a deep brown as to be almost black. She was a striking figure, wearing a grey travelling dress made tight to the throat, simple, but of excellent cut and cloth. The hands, rarely still, were particularly long and shapely, and she had long since taken to emphasising them by the wearing of several large and very heavy rings.

Her companion was less remarkable. A youth of but average height he sat in his corner a picture of dejection, his slightly myopic blue eyes fixed firmly on his costly and highly polished hessians. Unlike his mother, whose hair was as dark as a raven's wing, he had been blessed with a shaggy crop of almost colourless hair which despite the efforts of the various artists called to his assistance, never looked other than ragged. His jaw, too, lacked determination, tending to recede weakly into the intricate folds of his neckcloth, and his nose, far from being hooked, had an unfortunate tendency to turn up. He had even been a disappointment to his mother. A strong-willed woman, it had been a bitter blow to discover that the only offspring she was likely to produce had unfortunately decided to take after the gentleman she had some years previously bullied into marrying her. But she was nothing if not resourceful, and she had decided, within five minutes of being handed the tiny being swathed in a profusion of shawls and blankets that he should not fail through any fault of hers. So the unhappy Gerard had been sent away to school at the tender age of nine, since Lady Culcheth had no intention of coddling her child by having him educated in the comfort of his own home. He had loathed every minute of it, and when, at eighteen, he had finally hoped to be allowed to return home, his mother had shattered these dreams by announcing her intention of sending him to Oxford. But here even she could not prevail. No amount of tutoring could instil into Gerard the ability to pass Smalls, and Lady Culcheth had been forced to accept this setback as she had done all the rest.

Now she had other plans for her son's future. It was not until Daviot was almost within sight, however, that she chose to reveal her latest scheme for her son's felicity. With horror he turned to her, regarding her out of pale blue eyes fringed with a profusion of sandy lashes.

'Marry, Mama?' he echoed in dismay.

'Oh, indeed, Mama, must I?'

'Don't be nonsensical, Gerard,' said his mother briskly, turning to brush the lapels of his travelling coat with short sharp movements. 'You know very well what is expected of you, and if you must run into debt in that way it is only your duty to attempt to repay your Papa for his generosity. Lady Rosamund will make an excellent bride for you, and will succeed me very well.'

'Yes, Mama, I daresay, but won't she think it a trifle odd? I mean, my just popping the question like that?'

'Gerard, I sometimes wonder where these ridiculous notions of yours come from! Certainly not from me! Naturally she will not think it odd. She will doubtless be expecting it. However, you must be positive about these things, Gerard. You are too easily led. You must sweep her off her feet.'

'Yes, Mama,' said Gerard, a picture of dejection.

'Now,' continued her ladyship in

business-like accents, 'I have it on good authority that we will find Sir Hugh Eavleigh and Garvise at Daviot. This is of course unfortunate. We would have been better suited with just ourselves. However, Gerard, you will have an undoubted advantage over them both. You will one day be a peer, although, of course, we all hope your dear Papa will live many years more. But this is not something to be discredited, and you will kindly remember it in your dealings with Lady Rosamund. Then, Gerard, you are only twenty-one, which gives you an advantage of fifteen years or more over your rivals. What woman will choose an old man of nearly forty when there is someone of twenty-one perfectly willing? If you do as I say you will have no difficulty in persuading the lady to accept your suit. Now, to embrace the sister you must first embrace the brother.'

The Honourable Gerard Culcheth looked considerably alarmed and opened his mouth to protest. Lady Culcheth, perceiving misunderstanding in her offspring, forced herself to be patient and said: 'You will befriend Viscount Kearsley, Gerard. They are twins, you understand, and therefore close. You have an advantage over the Viscount of one year. You will therefore capture his respect.'

'Yes, Mama,' said the unfortunate Gerard, wondering desperately how this was to be achieved. 'How shall I do that, Mama?'

'Were you any normal boy I would suggest you impress him with your sporting prowess. However, that would be pointless. Deprived as you are of this I advise you to encourage the Viscount to confide in you. Teach him to be open, listen to him. You might amuse him with some tales of society if you chose. I presume you have some tales? Good. Young men, you know, Gerard, have a great respect for a man with a way with ladies, unaccountable though that is! You will therefore talk of your conquests, such as they are, but you must be careful, Gerard, not to boast. However, I believe I need not worry on that score. You must make an effort, Gerard. Take care with your dress. Do not be showy, but be elegant. Now, I wonder, can you do this?'

'Do I really have to, Mama? I would much rather just go home!'

For perhaps the thousandth time Lady Culcheth wondered how she managed to produce such a pathetic specimen for a son. She was calm, however, merely clicking her tongue and saying sharply: 'Nonsense! I have every reason to believe you will like Lady Rosamund. And remember, I shall be at your side throughout the visit doing what I can to ease your path. There is no mother, and I am hopeful of persuading Lady Rosamund to regard me in some sense in that light. Now, Gerard, tell me you understand.'

'I understand, Mama, but I do wonder sometimes whether you place too much confidence in my abilities.'

Since Lady Culcheth had no such

confidence she was able to reply quite calmly that he was talking nonsense, and draw his attention to the fact that they had just passed the Daviot lodge.

Harry greeted the news that the Culcheths had arrived with an announcement that he would be out to dinner. Rosamund, to whom this declaration was made in the library, made a half-laughing protest, saying: 'Indeed, Harry, you must not do so! Besides, wherever would you go?'

He winked at her and said nothing.

'Harry!' exclaimed his sister, horrified. 'You would not, would you? Think if you were caught!'

'My dearest sister, nothing would better dissuade these tiresome suitors of yours than to have you intimately acquainted with what is commonly known, I believe, as a bridle-cull!'

Rosamund laughed reluctantly, but said: 'Please, Harry, do not! Why are you not satisfied? I'm sure that disagreeable old woman from last night will inform against you.'

Harry shrugged, and sunk lower down in his chair, his long legs stretched out before him. 'And what if she does? They will never associate her tale of an uncouth ruffian with Viscount Kearsley, heir to Daviot!'

'Perhaps not, but the time must come, you know very well, when you will slip up! If only you would let me come, I should feel so much happier.'

Harry stood up at that and crossed the room with rapid strides. 'We've already discussed that, Ros! I cannot have you with me!'

'Very well, Harry, but I wish you would tell me why.'

He looked at her a moment, then moved to put an arm about her slim form. 'I cannot let you run the risk, little one. I appreciate your wanting to come, indeed I do, but I run risks enough without having to worry about protecting you.'

'So it is that!' she exclaimed, staring up at him anxiously. 'You are angry because I let you down!'

He laughed then, hugged her quickly and released her. 'Silly chit,' he said, not unkindly. 'You know I like having you with me! But the risks for you are so much greater! I could not guarantee that I could rescue you before your sex was discovered. My risks must be my own. After all, if I don't take care of you who will? Certainly not Papa, trying to foist you onto some poor deluded victim as he is.'

'Don't be unkind, Harry, please. I'm sure Papa only means it for the best.'

'Oh, undoubtedly,' responded Harry dryly, perching on one corner of the leather-topped desk. 'But he does not see how he mortifies you in the process, summoning all the dregs to marry you off!'

'Sir Hugh is not a dreg, Harry! I thought you liked him!'

He laughed. 'I do! And if he were not so old I might even think of furthering father's cause! But he's nearly an old man, Ros, you know he is.'

'You know nothing,' she retorted with a sudden and unexpected flash of irritation. She glared at him for a moment and then smiled. 'Oh Harry, do let me come! I shan't be so foolish again, you know.'

He shook his head. 'There's too much at risk for you,' he answered simply.

'Then stay at home yourself! You will only be caught one day, you know you will!'

'You worry too much,' he said, carelessly flicking one rosy cheek. 'Besides, you would not force me to meet your suitors, would you? It's more than I could endure! And just think, my love, without me they will have so much more opportunity to get to know you!'

'Oh, you are abominable!' she cried, giving him a fierce glare. Harry laughed and pulled one of her many ringlets.

He did not relent, and Rosamund found herself obliged to face her many suitors unprotected. The inclination to appear as unattractive as possible she had regretfully smothered, and appeared in a gown of white kerseymere with pearl buttons, her chestnut hair drawn into a knot on the top of her head with two curled locks falling over her ears. She had not been at the table many minutes before she discovered that one at least of the gentlemen in question did not regard the prospect of wedlock with unalloyed jubilation. The Honourable Gerard Culcheth, impeccably attired in knee breeches, dark blue coat and white waistcoat, his cravat intricately arranged in the style known as 'Waterfall', was seated, to his mother's disgust, next to the Earl, and really too far away for conversation with Lady Rosamund to be attempted. In spite of her ladyship's frequent glares and nods he applied himself studiously to his meal, refusing to ingratiate himself as his Mama had wished with the noble Earl of Carston. Lady Culcheth was a redoubtable female, however, and when she determined that there was little or nothing she could do about her son's disobedience at that moment she bent her mind to the more practical problems of winning her hostess's confidence.

Rosamund observed all this with amusement. Lady Culcheth tended to overpower, and while Rosamund, never having met the lady previously, was at first startled by her strident tones and piercing glare, she soon settled down to enjoy herself.

Across the table Sir Hugh observed the lady's progress with amusement. He was himself acquainted with this rather formidable female and was anxious to see how Rosamund, herself rarely at a stand, would cope with the new arrival. He considered his hostess speculatively over a large slice of delicate veal, and became aware gradually that Lady Culcheth was holding forth to her upon the Byron scandal. 'Of course,' she stated, 'Sally Jersey was a fool even to think that society would accept the fellow after that! One feels sorry for

Augusta, naturally, but if one half of what his unfortunate wife has said is true — !' She paused delicately.

Rosamund hesitated for a moment and then said: 'I cannot help but feel, Lady Culcheth, that had it been me I should have kept my own counsel.'

The older woman stared at her. 'Indeed!' she said after a moment. And then, in milder tones: 'Well, I daresay you might be right, my dear, Annabella Milbanke was doubtless a very imperfect wife for such a man. Brilliant, of course, although not quite in my style.' She turned her attention once more to her plate, and Rosamund gathered that the subject was now closed. She felt Sir Hugh's eyes upon her, and kept her own firmly lowered. In a moment, however, Lady Culcheth had turned to her again.

'It is such a pity you spend so little of your time in London,' she declared, fixing an eagle eye upon her hostess. 'Kean's 'Lear' really should not be missed! Can you not persuade the Earl to open up Grosvenor Place?'

'Perhaps, but it really would be most unfair upon him as he dislikes town so very much.'

'That is a great pity,' she stated, removing her gaze from Rosamund to fasten it upon Sir Hugh. 'Do you not agree, Sir Hugh? Do you not think Kean's 'Lear' a master-piece?'

He smiled at her. 'If you are speaking of the theatre, ma'am, I must admit to being completely without knowledge in that area. It is many years since I attended the Play.'

Lady Culcheth stared at him for an unblinking moment, clearly deemed his response unworthy of comment, and transferred her attention to her hostess. Sir Hugh glanced at Rosamund, but it was fortunate that her head was turned slightly away, otherwise each might have been overcome by unbecoming laughter.

The evening ended with whist for chicken stakes. At Lady Culcheth's instigation the table was set up and Garvise, Gerard and Rosamund summoned to play with her ladyship. Sir Hugh, finding himself unnecessary, unobtrusively wandered into the gardens, there to indulge in the warm air in what was perhaps his only vice. He had never cared for snuff, but an occasional cigar, when not offensive, suited him very well. He lit one now as he stood on the veranda, coolly sending up columns of smoke towards the stars.

He was enjoying his stay at Daviot more than he would have thought possible. He was fond of both Harry and Rosamund in a fatherly sort of way, and it had only taken the arrival of his old friend Garvise to make his contentment complete. The presence of Lady Culcheth and her son was, of course, dampening, for the Lady had an irritating way of talking to him as though he had one foot in the grave, but he felt he might reasonably bear this single blemish on his contentment. He was not surprised Harry had absented himself from dinner; in fact, he had half-expected Rosamund to be missing also, since his knowledge of her had led him to believe she had little time for social niceties. He did not realise it, but he was unconsciously relieved that Rosamund had after all some idea of social behaviour. The Earl had plainly been irritated by the fact that his son was not present, and had several heated and whispered exchanges with his daughter on the subject while they had waited for Lady Culcheth. Rosamund had obviously placated him, and he had been able to escort Lady Culcheth in to dinner with every appearance of complacency. Sir Hugh was not deceived, however. Lord Carston was grieved and hurt that his son had had so little regard for his wishes.

The party broke up early that evening. Lady Culcheth owned to tiredness, and Rosamund, who had no desire to keep her suitors lingering for longer than was necessary, followed her from the room.

Sir Hugh had been asleep for three hours or more when he was aroused by a soft scratching on the door. He was awake at once, and sat up, automatically straightening the white night-cap on his head.

'Who is it?' he called.

'It's me, Sir Hugh. May I come in?'

For a startled moment that baronet did nothing, and then he threw back the bedclothes and scrabbled hastily for the dressing gown on a nearby chair. Thus suitably attired he padded barefoot across the room to open the door. As he had thought Rosamund was there, fully clothed, holding up up a solitary candle.

'Did I waken you?' she asked unnecessarily. 'I'm sorry if I did, but indeed I must talk to you! I really don't know what to do!'

Sir Hugh gathered in an instant that something was amiss, and, after scouring the passage fleetingly, guided her into the room and shut the door.

'If your father hears of this he'll have my hide!' he whispered fiercely, taking the candle from her hand and applying it to the branch on the chest of drawers. 'I do hope you are not intending to make a habit of this!'

She smiled then, but said: 'Indeed, Sir Hugh, you may be certain I would not be here were it not absolutely necessary!'

He glanced at her, and said: 'Do I gather it is that scapegrace brother of yours?'

She nodded, her brown eyes large and anxious.

'I think you had better sit down, Lady Rosamund,' he said, indicating a large armchair near the window, 'and tell me just what this is about!'

She obeyed, noticing with relief that the window was uncurtained and that the moonlight afforded her a dim view of the gardens beneath. Sir Hugh pulled up a hard wooden chair and seated himself opposite her, his bare toes protruding from beneath the folds of his long brocade dressing gown. Lady Rosamund glanced at him, and, to his great consternation, giggled suddenly.

'Oh, forgive me, Sir Hugh, please, but do you think you could take off that silly night-cap? If I have to stare at it I shall never be able to tell you anything!'

Sir Hugh reddened but grinned, and pulled off the offending night-cap at once.

'Thank you! You have no idea how ridiculous they look on top of an earnest expression!'

Sir Hugh resolved never to wear one again.

'You are quite right,' she began, twisting her fingers anxiously in the folds of her gown, 'it is Harry. I don't suppose I need to tell you where he went this evening?' Sir Hugh shook his head. 'No, I thought not. Well, you see, as a rule he is home by midnight and if I'm not with him I wait up and let him in, just to be certain all is well. I worry dreadfully, you know, when I can't see what he's doing. Well, he has not returned! I checked in his room, too, just to see if he came in without my knowing, not that he would, but he's not there. I'm so worried. The latest he has ever been is half after one!'

Sir Hugh grunted. 'What time is it now?'

'Past three!'

Sir Hugh regarded her frowningly for a moment. 'Do you know where he went?'

'He didn't say, precisely, but he usually waits on the main Andover road. It takes quite a lot of traffic, particularly at this time of year when people are out of London.'

The baronet nodded thoughtfully. 'And I suppose you can think of only one reason why he should be late.'

'That he has been taken! Yes! Oh, I am so concerned! I did not know who to tell, either! Papa would be useless, besides being so angry, and hurt of course, so I decided to come to you, even though no virtuous female would even consider entering a gentleman's bedchamber, particularly at night! But then I knew I could trust you not to think badly of me, or at least, not to think any worse of me than you do at the moment!'

He chuckled at that, but said: 'My dear Rose, I don't know what you think I can do! Surely your father would be the proper person to consult?'

'But you don't understand! If I told Papa he would make no push to rescue Harry! He would simply say, quite sadly, you know, that Harry had come by his just deserts and we must abide by the judge's decision!'

Even Sir Hugh, who tended to regard the function of the law as unquestionable was inclined to think this view extreme, and said as much.

'Oh, but you do not understand Papa!' she exclaimed agitatedly. 'He would think it all a visitation, or some such thing!'

'Good God!' exclaimed Sir Hugh

blankly, staring at her.

'So you see, you must help me to rescue Harry! I am relying on you!'

Sir Hugh was by no means impervious to the charms of those beseeching brown eyes, but for the present he failed to see how he could be of service. Even in his youth he had never felt inclined to emulate the more madcap schemes of his contemporaries, such as partaking in curricle races or accepting without a blink a wager to ride backwards to Brighton, and now he tended to sit back and let the world get on with its idiocies as it chose. It seemed, however, that he was going to be embroiled whether he liked it or not, so he said: a trifle wearily: 'Where can Harry be?'

'Sir Joshua Kingman is the local Justice. There is a lock-up, I know, at Upavon Manor. Harry must be there.'

'Then I suppose I must saddle a horse without delay,' said Sir Hugh, attempting to banish all thought of his bed and be enthusiastic about a ride *ventre à terre* in the early hours of the morning.

'You will help me!' Rosamund jumped up joyfully and grasped his hands in hers. 'Oh, I am so grateful, you can have no conception! I knew you would not let us down. I'll go and change.'

She started for the door, but Sir Hugh stopped her. 'You don't have to do that, Rose.'

She laughed then. 'Surely you do not expect me to ride in this dress? Really, Sir Hugh!'

'Since I must go, child, I prefer to go alone. It is no business to involve you in.'

The brown eyes twinkled up at him mischievously. 'No, Sir Hugh, you do not exclude me from this adventure! Besides, you would never find Upavon Manor in the dark without me! I shall be ready in five minutes, Sir Hugh, and will meet you at the head of the stairs.'

5

There was a sharp breeze as they rode out across the grass of the Park. Scudding clouds occasionally obscured the moon, but the night was generally clear and light. Sir Hugh, entering into the mood of the affair, had donned his clothes with a haste and carelessness that would have shocked his fastidious valet, and had even gone so far as to knot a spotted kerchief about his neck. Even at thirty nine he was not unaware of the highly romantic nature of the whole affair, and could not but admit that he rather fancied himself as the knight errant Lady Rosamund seemed to think him. When he thought of his mission, however, he knew some misgivings.

Just what Rosamund had in mind he was uncertain, but it seemed likely that breaking into a justice's gaol and helping a highwayman to abscond would certainly feature in the catalogue for the night's entertainment. How this was to be achieved he was unsure, but he supposed, rather uneasily, that gaols were not fashioned for easy opening by the uninitiated. With an effort he banished a vision of himself dangling from the gibbet and tried to assume some of his companion's unconcern. Indeed, she seemed quite unaware of the dangers, riding perfectly calmly a little before him, dressed as before in her disreputable shirt and breeches.

'Just how active is your Sir Joshua in the execution of his duties?' Hugh asked her as he bent down to open a gate before them.

She smiled. 'He is quite officious, I am afraid, although he hasn't had much luck on catching our local villains. I understand the highways are positively infested, and that apart from us!' she added, encouraging her horse through the open gate.

Sir Hugh nodded. 'Then he is not

likely to be impressed by a story of an impetuous young cub trying his arm.'

'Not at all, I'm afraid! In fact, he is likely to be so overjoyed at having caught someone at last that he won't listen to any representations on poor Harry's behalf!'

'Then it looks as though we must try to get him out ourselves,' said Sir Hugh, sounding as decisive as he could. 'I suppose he will have had sense enough not to give his own name.'

Rosamund chuckled softly. 'It will give him great pleasure to lead them all a dance,' she said, her eyes sparkling at the thought. 'I only wish I could have been there!'

'Thank heaven you were not!' responded Hugh with great feeling.

Rosamund turned to him and smiled. 'How unkind it is of me to embroil you in our affairs! It is our own doing, after all. I should not blame you, you know, if you wanted nothing more to do with us after this!'

Sir Hugh was not exactly sure what

he wanted, but since he knew perfectly well that alienation from the young Daviots was not the foremost of his desires he was able to say quite sincerely: 'I want to help,' and leave it at that.

It was a five mile ride to Upavon, and when they were well clear of Daviot and its environs they skirted back to the road and proceeded at a canter along the grass verge. About two miles from Upavon, however, the night was disturbed by the sound of hooves proceeding at a fair pace, and, from what they could tell, on their own verge. They had slowed to a walk at this point in order to rest the horses, and the hooves were clearly discernible.

'We had better take care,' said Hugh, reining in for a moment. 'If we cross to the other verge he is not likely to see us, however.'

Accordingly they moved onto the road, but had barely reached the opposite verge before Rosamund, who had been staring hard into the darkness, suddenly said: 'I'm sure that's Harry!'

There was no reason for her to say so; the night was too dark and the horseman still too far distant for her to tell. Nevertheless she reined in her mount and stood in the middle of the road staring intently into the gloom.

'I know it's Harry!' she exclaimed, and, kicking up her mare, she started forward and called his name.

There was a startled exclamation, a scuffling and trampling of hooves, and Viscount Kearsley, his face impressively muffled, rose up before them out of the darkness.

'So it is you, Ros!' he exclaimed, astonished. 'What the devil are you doing here?'

'My dear Kearsley,' said Sir Hugh, who had previously gone unnoticed, 'so ungracious when we come to rescue you!'

'Sir!' Harry ejaculated, astounded. 'Ros, what have you been about?'

She laughed then. 'I have brought Sir

Hugh to help break you out of gaol! I was convinced you must have been caught. Harry, where have you been?'

'Oh, here and there,' he answered lightly, his eye on Sir Hugh's tall figure.

Sir Hugh smiled in the darkness. 'I collect by your wary manner, young man,' he said severely, 'that you are reluctant to reveal your doings while I am present. However, since I have been roused and dragged from my bed at some unheard-of hour, mounted and sent out on illegitimate activity all on your behalf I think the least you might do is explain how you came to be galloping about the countryside with perfect impunity!'

Harry grinned reluctantly. 'Very well, sir, since you phrase it so! But let's start back, shall we, I've had the devil of an evening!'

Accordingly they turned and the horses began walking slowly back towards Daviot. 'Do tell us, Harry,' begged Rosamund. 'I have been so concerned about you!'

'Well, at least you were in the right about that,' said Harry frankly. 'The truth is, I've lost my ring!'

Rosamund gasped, and Sir Hugh raised his brows in question.

'The Daviot emerald,' Harry explained. 'My grandfather put it into my father's keeping until my twentieth birthday. I've no idea of its value, except that it must be considerable.'

'But Harry, how did you come to lose it?'

He gave a short laugh. 'It was stolen from me.'

There was a silence, then Rosamund said: 'You will have to report it, and we must think of a way to explain what you were doing at this hour.'

'If only that were all, Ros!' He hesitated, and then said: 'The truth of it is, it seems I've run foul of some fellow called Chuffy Dick. I've had a run of luck recently. I found a splendid stretch of road, all trees and bushes, plenty of cover, and have really

106

had very little trouble. Last night was a true haul! However, tonight everything seemed fine. There was a fair moon, but plenty of cloud cover too, and as far as I could see no trouble. Mind you, if there weren't always the possibility of danger there would be little point in my doing it. But that's neither here nor there. Anyway, I had to wait nearly two hours before anything appeared, and then it was the most antiquated chariot you can imagine, drawn by a single pair. Well, I almost didn't stop it it was so dowdy, but by that time I was so bored I thought I might as well, and it was a good thing I did for such a board you have never seen! It was an old gentleman with a beard like Methusalah and a stick which he waved at the the slightest provocation. Nearly took my eye out, too! He had a chest, of all things, under the seat, jammed with rolls of soft! It must have been something nearing twenty thousand, at the very least! Then there was a gold watch, better than yours, sir,' he added with a grin, 'and a ruby ring the size of which you would not believe, square cut, like a lump of rock! I can tell you, Ros, I thought my luck well in! You should have seen the time I had strapping that cursed chest onto the back of the mare. Not that it was heavy, but a more awkward thing you've never seen! I did it in the end, though, and put the watch and ring in the pocket of my coat, all right and tight. You will be pleased to hear sir, that I had the courtesy to leave the old gentleman the few shillings he kept in his pocket! So there was I with a chest strapped to Sally's rump and my pocket stuffed with 'gewgaws', trotting along as pretty as you please, when up jumps a fellow from the bushes and points a pistol at my temple! I do not believe as long as I live, that anything will surprise me more.

"Oho,' says the fellow loudly, 'so here you are! Got the pretties nicely stowed, m'dear?'

'Well, I hardly knew what to say. But

it transpired that this was Chuffy Dick, and he had not come alone. It seems, my friends, as though I have been trespassing on his — er — grounds, and he was not too pleased about it! Well, the long and the short of it was, he took the chest, stripped me of my jacket, and found the ring and watch straight away. Wyton's snuff-box too, dash it. They were all set to be off, all four of them, when one spots the emerald on my hand which I, foolish for once, had omitted to remove. I know what you say, Ros, remove all distinguishing features! Well, you wanted to come with me, so I'm well served. They took it, of course, and my finger almost as well, and I must admit I feel lucky I'm not lying in the ditch with my throat cut.'

A pause followed this recital. At last Rosamund said: 'Harry, that is a dreadful thing!'

'Well, it was almost too much danger for me!' Harry admitted with a sudden grin. 'But it seems there's a certain code of honour among the Gentlemen, and although I apparently broke it by my act of trespass they had no intention of likewise demeaning themselves. In fact, they let me off without a scratch!'

'You were very lucky,' said Sir Hugh, gravely eyeing the young man beside him.

'I know it, sir,' Harry said at once, 'but the deuce of it is, how am I going to explain the loss of that cursed emerald? Father's bound to notice, seeing as how he always thought Grandpapa should have left it to him!'

'Really, Harry, that's hardly fair!' protested Rosamund at once.

'Stuff,' responded her twin. 'If I hadn't remembered to ask for it I swear he would never have handed it over. But that's neither here nor there. The thing is, I must recover the accursed thing, which is why I'm so late.'

'Oh Harry, have you got it then?'

'Of course I haven't, you goose! Do

you think I'd tell you all this if I had? I haven't, but it's not for want of the attempt, I can tell you!'

Rosamund eyed him suspiciously. 'What have you done?'

'I followed them,' said Harry, grinning. 'They tried to chase off Sally, but my little darling is too faithful to go far, and I caught her before they'd gone a hundred yards! So I followed them, discreetly, right back to a place called the Black Cock, an inn, over at Uppington. I thought I might be able to creep inside if I waited long enough but, would you believe it, they keep a look-out posted, and he didn't close his eyes once the whole time I was there!'

'So that's why you were so long!'

He grinned. 'I knew you'd fret, but what else could I do? I had to know where to find the thing, and besides, I had no idea you'd be foolish enough to rouse poor Sir Hugh!'

Poor Sir Hugh smiled and said: 'I

suppose your father will notice the ring is missing?'

'Oh, undoubtedly! If not all at once, then he will after a while. As I said, he really wanted it for himself and it annoyed him to be passed over in that fashion!'

Sir Hugh nodded and rode on in thoughtful silence. 'I do not presume, Kearsley,' he said eventually, 'that you intend to let this go?'

'The devil I do!' responded the Viscount instantly. 'But I would much rather you did not concern yourself with our problems, sir. My sister was wrong to have roused you.'

'Afraid I shall have something to say on the matter, you young cub?' Hugh demanded pleasantly.

'Far from it,' responded Harry at once. 'My only worry is that you will advise me to tell my father everything.'

Sir Hugh smiled slightly. 'In that you are right!'

'I thought as much! Sir, this is not your trouble! I beg you will stand back from us! We are as we are, you know, and nought will change us. I shall think of a way.'

'That, my dear Kearsley, is precisely what I am afraid of.'

It was after five o'clock when they finally led their mounts quietly into the cobbled stable yard. No representations on the part of Sir Hugh or his sister would persuade the Viscount either to reveal what he had in mind or to confess his dealings to his father. Accordingly Sir Hugh sought his bed in great uneasiness, certain he would find it impossible to sleep. At his habitual hour of eight o'clock, however, his now rather nervous valet peered round the door to discover his master in deep slumber, and consequently withdrew for another couple of hours.

The excitement of the night before seemed to have had no effect on the twins when they appeared later that morning. They were as light and careless as ever, and greeted the information that a toad had been discovered in the Honourable Gerard Culcheth's bed the previous evening with bland and innocent stares. No one could conceive how the creature had come to be there, and the housemaid, when summoned, swore on her Bible that the bed had been empty when she had turned it down. But it was an unfortunate business. Gerard, it transpired, had no love for toads, and, when he all but put his foot on it, had let out such a scream that his mother had descended on him with demands to know what he meant by disturbing the household. Lady Culcheth, although angered by the affair and clearly blaming Harry, had no sympathy for her son, who, she announced, should simply have thrown the creature out of the window with the contempt it deserved. It was quite apparent, however, that her enjoyment of her stay had been lessened by the incident, and Gerard's, never strong, completely demolished.

'So,' said Sir Hugh, encountering his

hostess in the shrubbery that afternoon, 'the unfortunate Gerard does not like toads!'

She laughed and said: 'I truly cannot imagine how it came to be there!'

'Can you not, indeed! I believe Lady Culcheth has some pretty shrewd ideas on the subject!'

'I know, but they are quite wrong.'

He raised his brows. 'Are they? Surely you are not trying to tell me Harry is not responsible?'

She raised her eyes to his and said: 'He is not, I am afraid. In fact, I have a confession to make.'

'It was not you!' He sounded appalled.

She nodded, and laughed. 'Do you think me very dreadful? Yes, of course you must! It was I! Harry bet me I would not do it, so what could I do but accept?'

Sir Hugh smiled, but said: 'You might have known it would be badly received.'

'I rather think that was Harry's plan,'

she said ruefully. 'I'm sure I can tell *you*, sir, that Harry does not like what Papa is doing. He would far rather it were left up to me!'

They had been walking, but Sir Hugh stopped now, and turned to face her. 'You have only to say, you know, and I will leave, and take Garvise too if I can manage it.'

She flushed fierily and said: 'But of course I didn't mean you! Did you think I could be so impolite?' She looked at him for a moment and then said: 'Yes, I see you did Sir Hugh, forgive me, it was badly done.'

Taking her hand he drew it within his arm. 'What a ridiculous child you are! You could not offend me. I do not have to pretend I don't know why I was invited, or why the others are here. But you may be certain that for my part you will not be pestered by attentions that are unwelcome. I give you my word.' He released her arm, and stood smiling down at her.

Rosamund hesitated, and then said:

'Thank you! And I do pray you will not leave! Harry has so enjoyed having your company, and as for me, well, I shall always be grateful you came with me last evening!'

'Ah, yes. Tell me, Lady Rosamund, has your disreputable brother come up with any equally disreputable plans of late?'

She laughed, and shook her head. 'No, but he will, of that you may be sure! He certainly will not let Chuffy Dick keep the emerald, I know. I hope, Sir Hugh, that you will not concern yourself with our problems. They are ours, you know, and for us to solve.'

'Of that I make no doubt but I do beg of you, if ever you find yourself in trouble, not to hesitate to come to me. I may not be well versed in the way of life your Harry prefers, but I might be able to help when even Harry cannot.'

She smiled gratefully at him and said: 'Thank you, Sir Hugh, I will not forget.' Then she curtseyed, and made her way back to the house. Sir Hugh watched her go, then turned, and wandered up towards the woods in search of Jeremy Garvise.

6

He found his friend in earnest contemplation of the house, standing on the prominence from which Sir Hugh had observed Mr. Garvise's arrival.

'I am trying to decide,' he said, 'on the date of this house. I thought at first it was all one period, but now I can see quite plainly that the East wing, ours, I fancy, is of a later date. The slates, you notice, are not quite so weathered, and the stone, too, is altogether less grey.'

Together they subjected the edifice to their scrutiny, and after a few minutes Sir Hugh was able to agree with his friend's pronouncement.

'I saw you with the little Rosamund,' said Garvise, as they turned from the object of their contemplation. 'Has she confessed to her brother's part in the toad?'

'It seems, Jerry, as though his part

was a wager. The little Rosamund was responsible.'

Garvise gave a bark of laughter but said: 'It seems the little lady does not love our presence.'

'No more she does,' he admitted, 'but I believe the brother likes it less.'

'That young puppy! He needs a stiff hand, Hugh! Such a performance last evening, and never an apology today! Whoever heard of a son missing dinner on the guests' first evening, and without even the slimmest excuse!'

'He is bored merely. The Earl should take them both to London. He would wear it out soon enough.'

'Do you think so? In my opinion he needs employment. Like as not he'd take to gaming in town.'

Sir Hugh considered a moment, and then said: 'The Army, perhaps? Do you know, Jerry, I believe you could be right. It would be better, at least, than ending his days on a gibbet. But the Earl, I believe, would have none of it.'

'More fool he, then,' said Garvise, carelessly swiping the grass with his cane.

'However, I wish I might persuade him to countenance such a visit. What he needs is a few friends, Jerry. He depends too much on his sister for company.'

'And she on him?' Garvise cocked an inquiring eyebrow at his friend.

'Not so much. I believe she realises their relationship cannot continue for ever.'

'And what of you, Hugh? What is your position in all this?'

The baronet looked surprised. 'Mine? I have none!'

'If that is true then I am much mistaken.'

Sir Hugh smiled reluctantly. 'Damn you, Jerry, why do you have to be so cursed perceptive?'

'Don't take much, old fellow, I'm afraid. Just have to look at you, after all. Why do you not take her?'

He gave a short laugh. 'Faith, Jerry,

I'm an old man to them.'

'To the boy, perhaps, but the lady gives no sign that she thinks so of you.'

'She does, however. Were I so much as to hint at anything other than a paternal interest she would withdraw from me at once.'

Jeremy Garvise glanced sideways at his friend but said merely: 'How long have you known?'

Sir Hugh did not pretend to misunderstand. 'About half an hour, damn it!'

Garvise chuckled. 'All these years, and you're done for by a wild bit like that! You must be mad, my dear Hugh!'

'I might as well be for all the good it'll do!'

'Don't discount your charms, old fellow. Since you've taking to wearing that rakish neck-cloth they have increased ten-fold!'

Rosamund found her brother in the armoury. Grasping a buttoned foil he was pacing the gallery floor, impressively lunging and parrying an imaginary foe at spasmodic intervals. On his sister's entrance he turned to her, swept several ferocious strokes at her slim form, and then stopped, resting the tip of his foil on the floor.

'Good morrow, ma'am,' he said, bringing up the foil in an exaggerated salute. 'And how is the noble Hugh?'

'Concerned about you, Harry, I'm afraid. He thinks you're planning something dangerous.'

'And so I am, m'dear, so I am! Time runs short!' He lunged sharply again, bringing the button to rest on the bodice of Rosamund's blue crepe morning dress. 'Such a plan I have devised, and simple, m'dear, with your help.'

She smiled. 'I thought as much! Harry, you are incorrigible! What would you have me do?'

'Tell me, my love, how proficient would you be as a housemaid?'

Rosamund gave no sign of horror,

merely wrinkling her brow in thought. 'Pretty bad, I should imagine. Must it be a housemaid? I might be better in the kitchen.'

Harry grinned. 'Doubtless, my dear, but it is a housemaid I stand in urgent need of.'

'At the Black Cock, of course. Yes, I see. Well, I could try, of course, though I don't guarantee to last it out above sennight.'

'Which should be sufficient! First, however, you must acquire a bout of influenza.'

'But I've never had influenza in my life!' protested Rosamund, laughing.

'Dearest, since the only thing you have ever contracted is a mild bout of measles this cannot be helped. Influenza it must be.'

'Yes, but Harry, it will not be easy! Betty will help me, I know, but how can we prevent Nurse from trying to help?'

'That is a problem, I must admit. You must just leave her to me. You know I can turn her round my little finger.'

Rosamund smiled. 'It is to be hoped you can, Harry, indeed! Well, shall you write my reference, or shall I write my own?'

'Write your own, m'dear, I think. After all, it is hardly a gentleman's affair!'

It was at dinner that evening that Lady Rosamund first complained of the headache. As Lady Culcheth pointed out, too, she was remarkably pale, which pronouncement caused Harry, for one, to exclaim that he hoped she was sickening for nothing. Lady Rosamund replied in a husky little voice that she was sure she would be better in the morning, and continued to eat her meal. The pallor, which was, in fact, provided by a fine and careful dusting of flour from the kitchens, continued, however, and shortly before nine o'clock Rosamund excused herself on account of the headache which had, she said, grown unaccountably worse. Lady Culcheth declared that a good night's sleep would see her well, and on this heartening note Rosamund bade the company goodnight. Only Sir Hugh had remained silent, and on Rosamund's exit cast a long and speculative look at Harry, who returned it with a bland smile.

In the morning, however, Rosamund proved to be far from better. In fact, she was so indisposed that she could see no one but her brother and her maid, to the consternation of her old and faithful nurse, Mrs. Purnell. Nurse Purnell had cosseted the twins since their earliest years, and to be excluded now from attending her darling was very hurtful. She tried to persuade the Viscount to summon the doctor, but Harry was adamant in this. Rosamund, it seemed, wanted nothing but to be left alone.

For two days the situation continued, then, as almost everyone was partaking of a light luncheon in the smaller dining room Nurse Purnell, her starched cap askew and several strands of grey hair about her face, erupted onto the scene with the startling announcement that Lady Rosamund was not in the house.

The news was greeted by a stunned silence. No one knew what to say. Then the Earl, after glancing round at the astonished faces of his guests, rose, and said: 'Will you excuse me, please. Harry, a word with you.'

Sir Hugh's eyes were fixed on the young man's face, and what he saw there convinced him that the Viscount had had a definite part in Rosamund's disappearance. Harry's expression was one of innocent astonishment, but those eyes, so dark and expressive, were pregnant with mischief. Hugh said nothing, however, merely addressing himself once more to the cold tongue.

Lady Culcheth, however, was not so easily satisfied. Her eagle eyes had detected the panic latent in Nurse Purnell's agitated expression, and the slight look of mischief that Viscount

Kearsley had given Sir Hugh had also not gone unremarked. Accordingly she stood up, a tall, impressive woman, and said: 'Do I understand, my lord, that your daughter is not after all indisposed?'

Nurse Purnell cast an agonised look at her master, but Harry, for some reason not disinclined to conduct the interview in the presence of guests, said: 'Indeed, Father, they will have to know before long!'

The Earl glanced sharply at his son, and Lady Culcheth, still standing, said; 'What, pray, do you mean, young man?'

'Indeed, ma'am,' returned Kearsley at his most innocent, 'it is not for me to say!'

'Cut line, Harry,' said his father sharply, 'and tell us why your sister is not in her chamber.'

The brown eyes opened wide. 'Indeed, Papa, you do not know?'

At this Nurse Purnell, who had been following the conversation with her jaw slightly lowered, wailed. 'Oh, never say so! Oh, the naughty thing! That she should do it and not tell me!'

Lady Culcheth's piercing eyes snapped. 'Do I gather, my lord, that your daughter has *eloped*?'

The Earl cast a look of entreaty at his son, but Harry, did not perceive it, being engaged in studying the carving about the empty fireplace. He was forced to speak. 'Harry, tell us what you know of this.'

'Indeed, Papa, I am surprised you are unaware! You should have known you could not force Rosamund's hand in this way. If only you would agree to her marrying where she chooses!'

'And just who, young man, does she choose?' demanded Lady Culcheth in icy tones.

Harry cast a pained look of entreaty at his parent but the situation was now beyond his control and he merely shook his head wretchedly.

'I am waiting, Kearsley,' said her ladyship sternly.

'Well, my lady, it is Will James.'

'And who, may I ask, is Will James?'

'I believe, ma'am,' returned the Viscount blandly, 'that he was employed in our stables.'

'The *stables*?' echoed Lady Culcheth, while Lord Carston looked as though he would have an apoplexy.

'Do I gather,' he demanded angrily, 'that you have had the impudence to *encourage* your sister in this — this foolishness?'

'If you mean was I a party to their plans, sir, yes I was, but I was sworn to secrecy.'

The Earl of Carston opened his mouth to speak but Lady Culcheth interposed, saying: 'My lord, you will not be wishing us here at this time. Come, Gerard, we will assemble our possessions,' with which she breezed past the Earl, the Honourable Gerard meekly in her wake.

'I, too, my lord, should take my leave,' said Garvise with a slight bow. 'If my friend Eavleigh will bear me company we will not inconvenience you any longer than we need.'

The Earl made a half-hearted attempt to persuade his guests to stay but was plainly relieved when both politely declined. Once upstairs, however, Garvise turned to Sir Hugh and said: 'What sort of game is that young cub playing, I wonder?'

'I wish I knew!' Hugh said. 'What is certain is that she has not eloped.'

'So much I realised,' responded Garvise grimly. 'Devil's business, my friend?'

'That is sure! I only hope she is not in any physical danger.'

Garvise raised his brows. 'Surely, Hugh, he would not permit her to risk her life?'

'Would he not, indeed! Has he not just put her reputation into the greatest jeopardy?'

They had by this time reached Garvise's room, and Sir Hugh followed him in to drop immediately into an armchair.

'One thing is certain, at least,' he said, sinking low into the chair. 'I shall not leave the area until I know where she is.'

'Have you some idea?'

'I have. Besides, her brother is party to her scheme.'

'You should watch that young cub, Hugh. He's truly a wild one. There's no saying what he might not be about.'

'I tell you, Jerry, to think of what he could be doing makes my blood run cold!' He stood up, mechanically smoothing his sleeves. 'I must instruct that fellow of mine to pack up, but first it's young Kearsley I want to see!'

He found him without difficulty. As he reached the head of the stairs the door to the small dining room opened and the Earl marched out, his face white and strained, and disappeared down the passage. Harry appeared in the doorway, and, catching sight of the baronet, grinned amicably.

'I want a word with you, Kearsley,'

said Hugh, running down the stairway to meet him.

'With me, sir?' repeated the young man, his expression one of innocent bewilderment.

In answer Sir Hugh caught him by the arm and propelled him down the passage and into the open. 'I want to know, you young cub, where is your sister!'

'Indeed, sir,' responded Kearsley righteously, 'you must know I cannot tell you that! They have sworn me to secrecy.'

'You must think me remarkably foolish! Let me tell you, I have a suspicion that if I were to search for a certain Black Cock inn I would not find your sister far distant!'

Harry grinned. 'Your suspicions are of course your own, sir,' he said.

'Damn you!' said Sir Hugh explosively. 'I'll have this without roundaboutation, if you please! Where is your sister?'

Harry eyed him speculatively for a moment, and then said: 'Oh, I suppose you may as well know. Like as not you'd only interfere, and the Lord knows what that would do! She's working as a housemaid at the Black Cock. Has been these two days.'

'Good God!' exclaimed Sir Hugh, aghast. 'Do you seriously mean you have sent your sister into that den of vice? Has it not occurred to you what sort she will meet with?'

'Of course! That's why she is there, isn't it, to get my ring back?'

'Don't misunderstand me, Kearsley! You know very well what I mean! I tell you this, young man, if I find anyone has so much as laid a finger on your sister I shall take great pleasure in handing you to the Authorities!'

'Oh, I shouldn't do that, sir, if I were you. How do you think Rosamund would greet the news that her beloved brother had been turned over for hanging by his friend?' He paused a moment to let this sink in, and then said: 'Besides, Rosamund is not my sister for nothing. She can fence, and shoot as well as any man, and can give a good account of herself. It's a persistent man that takes liberties with my Ros!'

'I only hope, young man, that you are proved in the right of it!'

'For my own sake, of course, eh, Sir Hugh?' said Harry, his brown eyes twinkling mischievously.

Sir Hugh gave him a darkling look. 'Indeed! Now tell me, what does your father propose to do about this elopement tale?'

Harry seemed genuinely surprised. 'Do, sir? Why, nothing! What can he do, after all? He has no idea where they have gone, and besides, they have been two nights absent!'

'Do you seriously mean to tell me that your father intends to do nothing about it? That your sister could genuinely abscond and he would not act?'

Harry shrugged. 'It seems to me typical. He has washed his hands of us. I doubt, if she returned now, whether he would receive her.'

Sir Hugh kept his hands to himself with difficulty. 'And you talk so calmly! Do you not realise what you have done? Is your sister's reputation worth so little?'

'What does it matter if the world thinks things of her? She is still the same person, and that is all that matters to me.'

'Ay, to you, but what of her? What of her chances now should she indeed wish to marry?'

Harry laughed. 'Marry, sir? She will not marry! What need has she for others when she has me?'

Sir Hugh began to wonder how he could ever have liked the young man at all. 'You will take me to your sister today!' he said, his voice throbbing with barely suppressed anger.

Harry shrugged. 'If you wish. My father has permitted me to look for her. Though you will find Rosamund thinks exactly as I do.'

Sir Hugh said merely: 'I suppose

there is a Will James?'

'Oh yes! He ran off last week for no apparent reason.'

Sir Hugh nodded and started back to the house.

7

With his luggage bound for the Bull at Marlborough Sir Hugh set out late that afternoon for the Black Cock in the neighbourhood of Uppington. It proved to be a ride of some ten miles or more, and over some very rough and uncomfortable territory. Harry took the route by which he had followed Chuffy Dick and his companions, and it therefore skirted every highway and village of note. Harry had arranged to meet his sister that evening in the woods behind the few cottages that constituted Uppington, and they had waited only twenty minutes before they saw her white cap bobbing towards them across the grass. It was nearly dark and no moon was promised, but they saw her quite clearly and were able to step out and greet her. When she saw her brother Rosamund breathed a sigh of relief.

'Oh, Harry, I am so glad you are here! I think Mrs. Ditton is suspicious of me, and I'm sure she thinks I've run out to meet some village yokel! Which is no more than I have, of course!' She stood on tiptoe to kiss her brother's lean cheek, and her eye fell on Sir Hugh. 'So, Harry has confided in you, I see!'

Sir Hugh bowed. 'He has, my lady, but not without some persuasion. Perhaps, Kearsley, you should tell your sister just how she stands at present with the world.'

She turned inquiring eyes upon her brother who grinned and said: 'I've rid us of your suitors, m'dear!'

'You have! Oh Harry, how clever of you!' Her gaze clouded a second and she scanned his face anxiously. 'Harry, you didn't tell them about . . . about yourself?'

He laughed, and flicked her cheek. 'No, love, but Sir Hugh will have it

I've ruined you for life!'

'Good gracious! Well, do please tell me before I die of suspense!'

'I told them merely that you had eloped with one of the stable hands.'

Rosamund gave a choke of laughter but said: 'I understand Sir Hugh's consternation! Really, Harry, you will have me to a nunnery before I am much older!'

'Stuff!' said Harry roundly. 'You are still Lady Rosamund Daviot and always will be.'

'I'm afraid that will probably turn out to be all too true,' said Rosamund, eyeing her brother with an amused smile. 'Who do you think will take me now that I am . . . er . . . *fallen*?'

Harry made an irritated movement. 'Why all this talk of marriage? Indeed you are as bad as Sir Hugh!'

She gave the baronet a quick glance and said: 'Well, don't worry! If the worst comes about we must just persuade my last remaining suitor to take me as I am!' As soon as she said it she sensed a stiffening in the tall comfortable figure of Sir Hugh, but although she looked sharply up at him it was too dark to observe his exact expression. 'I suppose,' she said, turning to her brother, 'that you did not think to tell Papa the truth?'

'Well,' conceded Harry, 'I considered it a moment but it seemed such an opportunity to be rid of those fellows!'

She smiled, but said: 'I only hope Papa is not too worried.'

'He will only worry about how it will affect him,' replied her brother.

'I do hope so, indeed.'

'But what of the ring, Ros?' said Harry, who had been growing impatient.

Rosamund shook her head. 'I haven't got it yet, I'm afraid. He's been wearing it on his left hand, if you credit it, and seems as proud as Punch!'

'Damn his impudence!' exclaimed Harry, slapping his hand against his thigh in annoyance.

'Well, at least we know he hasn't sold it,' Rosamund pointed out logically.

'I suppose you haven't been able to get into his room at all?' Harry inquired not very hopefully.

She shook her head. 'He spends so little time there, and I thought it best not to be too bold all at once.'

Harry nodded thoughtfully. 'I suppose that is best,' he conceded.

'I had much rather she were never so bold,' Sir Hugh remarked dryly.

She raised her brows at him in surprise. 'Do you disapprove, then, of what I am doing?'

'Of course he does,' said Harry scornfully. 'Our friend turns out to be devilish straight-laced!'

'So I should hope,' retorted the baronet, 'when it comes to an affair like this! You seem to have no idea of what your sister might be exposed to!'

Harry opened his mouth to protest but Rosamund said quickly: 'Have you really been concerned? I am sorry. You shouldn't worry, you know. They are all quite nice people really. In fact I've only had one . . . er . . . improper advance so far, and he was so drunk he could hardly stand.' She laughed, but Sir Hugh seemed far from appeased. She realised this and said seriously: 'Very well. I promise you, sir, that I shall leave the instant things seem to be out of control and let Harry get his ring back on his own.'

'Well, thank you!' said Harry, by no means pleased.

'Oh come, it was your own fault, after all!'

Since this was true there seemed very little Harry could say, and he stood silent.

'Well,' said Rosamund, after a moment, 'since you are here, Harry, I suppose we had better see what we can do about this ring. Dick is out at the moment, I'm afraid, so perhaps we could wait for him to come home.'

Harry thought for a moment and then said: 'If he is out it is obvious where he is, is it not? I would prefer to waylay him as he returns, if you are with me, Ros.'

'Of course I am,' she started to say, but Hugh interrupted her.

'If you need help, Kearsley, I had rather you took me. Your sister should not be involved in such things.'

'Do you really think you can stop me?' she asked, looking up at him inquiringly.

'If I had my way I would lock you in the cellar until this was over!' he answered her roughly.

Rosamund seemed at a loss for a reply, but Harry, having stared open-mouthed at the baronet for a moment, suddenly said: 'Stap me if I don't take you with me, sir! After all,' he added seriously, 'this is hardly a task for you, Ros, you know.'

She looked from one to the other, and then said: 'Gentlemen, if you think you can exclude me now you are much mistaken!'

'Faith, Ros, how will you ride in that dress?'

'Faith, brother, I came prepared!' The the horror of the gentlemen she

144

immediately lifted her rough brown skirt and revealed her legs, properly cased in a pair of buff breeches.

Sir Hugh made a choking sound and Viscount Kearsley, a smile on his lips, said: 'I think she has us, sir, this time! Very well, minx, you may come, but only if you have a horse.'

'Of course I have a horse,' said Rosamund, seemingly put out by the suggestion that she should come thus unprepared.

'Then fetch the beast and meet us at the cross roads, that is if you can saddle it yourself.'

Rosamund cast her brother a fulminating glance and strode off without another word.

'Do you know, Kearsley, I think you have your hands full there.'

'I believe you are right,' responded the brother with a grin. 'In fact, I'm beginning to wonder if I was right to chase off her prospective husbands!'

It was some little time before Rosamund put in an appearance at the cross roads and both gentlemen were feeling decidedly weary by the time her little mare came trotting up the track towards them.

'I had some trouble with the man they keep posted,' she explained as she joined them at last. 'I think he suspected me of something, and I had rather a difficult task persuading him to let me go. In fact,' she added thoughtfully, 'I think he might expect something of me when I get back.'

Harry rolled his eyes heavenwards but Sir Hugh said immediately: 'Then there is no question of your returning!'

'Well, I must admit,' responded Rosamund as they moved off together, 'I think it might be a little awkward for me if I were to go back, but what happens if we do not recover the ring?'

'Whatever happens,' Harry pointed out, 'you will be unable to return since Dick is bound to recognise you after tonight.'

'Yes, he is, isn't he,' agreed

Rosamund, sounding somewhat relieved.

For some little time Harry had been fumbling in his pocket but now he gave a satisfied grunt and pulled out what looked like a bundle of rags. 'It's a good thing I came prepared for anything,' he said, examining carefully what he held. 'Here you are, Ros, and one for you too, sir.'

Mystified Sir Hugh received the strip of black material and scrutinised it curiously. 'Good God! It's a mask!'

Harry grinned. 'Do you want to be known, then? I certainly do not!'

Sir Hugh smiled. 'No, but I did not envisage this!'

'If I were you I would wear it,' Harry said seriously. 'You never know when Chuffy Dick might come on you again.'

Sir Hugh looked struck, but it was with some reluctance that he tied the mask over his eyes. Then, the black strip in place, he gave a little chuckle and shook his head.

Rosamund had discovered, during

her short stay at the Black Cock, that Chuffy Dick preferred to operate in an area approximately two miles south of Viscount Kearsley's position. The exact location varied from day to day, but Dick, it seemed, was a creature of habit, and having discovered a suitable place preferred to remain there. Accordingly it was towards the main Andover road that they directed their mounts, to wait until Dick's business should be concluded for the night. When the road was barely a quarter of a mile away Kearsley reined in and communicated in a hushed whisper that it would be better to dismount and leave the horses tethered while they discovered precisely where the highwayman was waiting. As a result of this statement a short argument ensued between the twins. Harry was wishful to leave his sister guarding the horses while he and Sir Hugh discovered Dick's where-abouts. Rosamund, however, greeted this unenthusiastically. Had she not, she demanded, been involved from the beginning? Was it not because Harry had forbidden her to go that he was in this fix at all? He had not scrupled, she noticed, to send her into the lion's den when it suited him, but now that he had the situation, apparently, under control, he no longer had any need for her but as some sort of glorified stable lad. And if he left her behind, she announced, there was a distinct possibility that neither she nor the horses would be there on his return. In vain did Harry call upon Sir Hugh for support. It had been plain to the baronet from the start who would prevail, and he watched their bickering with a faint smile of amusement on his lips.

Chuffy Dick was not difficult to find. Harry's instinct for good cover led him infallibly to a heavy clump of bushes and although they could see nothing the faint clink of a horse rolling its bit came unmistakably towards them, accompanied by an occasional snuffle as the horse shifted its position in the undergrowth. They were about to return for the horses when Harry, who had been crouched close to the ground, suddenly raised his hand in a silent warning. Sir Hugh watched brother and sister stiffen and exchange glances, and gathered therefore that something was amiss.

'Get down,' hissed the Viscount fiercely as the baronet started to ask what was the matter. 'Don't utter a sound, but keep your eye on the road, there's a carriage coming.'

Accordingly Sir Hugh, wondering what he was becoming involved in and feeling certain he would regret it in the morning, dropped full length onto the ground beside the twins and focused his eyes with difficulty on the road before him. For a while he was certain Harry had been mistaken and that no coach would appear, but just as his legs started to stiffen from the awkwardness of his position there came the unmistakable rumble of wheels over stone. An inner feeling urged him to get away while he still could and he very nearly tapped Harry on the shoulder. It was the thought of how feeble-hearted he would seem in the young man's eyes that made him hesitate and finally shake his head.

The pace of the carriage was not great and it was some time before it came sufficiently close to be visible against the dark sky. There was no sound from the covert beside them and for a hopeful moment Sir Hugh wondered if Dick had decided to leave this particular traveller alone. When the carriage was almost abreast of them however there was a loud explosion at very close proximity and a horse leapt directly into the path of the oncoming carriage, causing it to swerve violently across the road as the coachman heaved hard upon the reins. The team within the shafts leapt and snorted, some pulling frantically against the pressure of the brakes, and one of the leaders trying to back into the animals behind him. Within a moment the traces were inextricably tangled and the coachman was so involved in trying to pacify his team that he had no time to spare for the ominous black figure before him.

Apparently satisfied that the coachman was not going to do anything foolhardy Chuffy Dick urged his mount forward to come abreast of the vehicle. 'All right, m'dears,' said the highwayman gruffly, 'let's 'ave yer walubles, sharpish!'

What happened next was certainly unexpected. No sound came from within the carriage which was quite empty. Instead two mounted persons sprang from the opposite side of the road and from a position dangerously close to the twins and Sir Hugh two more persons emerged on foot, the foremost of whom declared: 'Stand, in the name of the King!'

Suddenly all was confusion. The coachman left his plunging team to their own devices and leapt down from his box with a large blunderbuss pointed convincingly towards the highwayman. The militia likewise produced weapons and Chuffy Dick appeared to be surrounded. All was not yet lost, however. With an oath the highwayman spurred his horse forward and leapt directly at one of the mounted men, exploding a pistol as he did so vaguely in the direction of the figure. There was a cry, and the soldier slumped onto the neck of his horse, one hand clasped to his shoulder.

'Good God!' exclaimed Harry, jumping up suddenly. 'We must help him!'

For a confused moment Sir Hugh thought Harry was running in aid of the wounded soldier and cursed his impetuosity. Then to his horror the young man grasped the arm of the soldier nearest to him who had been starting towards his companion, swung him round, and floored him with a neat right to the jaw. Within a second Rosamund too was on her feet, a large stick menacingly clasped, and started towards the foray. Sir Hugh had a fleeting vision of himself in irons, then he was on his feet and plunging towards the road.

For a moment he could identify no one among the collection of persons that littered the road. Chuffy Dick had been pulled from his horse by one of the soldiers, and two terrified animals were starting and snorting in the middle of the struggling group of people. One soldier lay prone on the ground and another was staggering about with his hand clasped tightly to his shoulder. Then Hugh distinguished Rosamund. A third soldier had her captive, and was marching her with her hands pinioned behind her towards the dark shape of the waiting carriage. Sir Hugh hesitated no longer. He leapt into the foray, clenched his fist, and planted a heavy punch in the small of the soldier's back. There was a loud groan, and Rosamund, finding the grip on her hands suddenly lessened, wrenched herself free and turned in time to see Sir Hugh deliver a sharp left to the unfortunate man's nose.

'Fetch the horses!' Sir Hugh fairly barked at her as she stood hesitating in the road. For a second she looked at him, then she nodded and darted off, skilfully avoiding a fallen soldier who made a lunge for her ankles as she passed. Satisfied that she had gone Sir Hugh turned once more to the struggling collection of men, trying in vain to distinguish the Viscount in all the confusion. For a second he thought he saw him, then a weight threw itself on him from behind and he found himself flat upon the rough ground, completely winded, with something large and heavy on the centre of his back.

'Leastways, you're not going any-wheres,' pronounced a voice roughly as his hands were pulled behind him and held painfully and firmly across his back. There came the sound of rending material, then a makeshift rope was wrapped tightly and skilfully about Sir Hugh's wrists. The headlines in the *Gazette* loomed large in his

155

imagination: 'Baronet to hang for highway robbery'. The pressure from his back was removed and an arm dragged him up. For a second he confronted the soldier who held him, and then a sudden pain flooded his skull and he slumped forward senseless to the road.

8

Gathering his fast ebbing strength Harry wrenched himself free from the arms that held him. A sharp blow to the stomach incapacitated his captor sufficiently to allow Harry to glance round quickly for the baronet. He had already seen Rosamund hurry away and had silently thanked Sir Hugh for his foresight. Now he was just in time to see Sir Hugh succumb to a sharp blow on the head and with an oath looked round for a suitable weapon. He found it in the shape of the blunderbuss which had been dropped early in the fray. Grasping it by the long wide barrel he tested its weight for a second, then strode purposefully towards the man who was even then dragging Sir Hugh in the direction of the carriage. Raising the clumsy weapon above his head he brought it down with force

157

at the juncture of neck and shoulder, causing the soldier to jerk sideways and down to the rough ground. There was an immediate exclamation and Harry glanced up in time to see a figure in the doorway of the coach. Then he had his hands beneath Sir Hugh's shoulders and was dragging his heavy and inanimate form across the road. The soldier in the carriage gave a harsh laugh.

'Too late, my friend, too late!' He jumped down into the road and marched purposefully to where Harry was desperately heaving on the dead weight.

'Stop where you are!' came a voice, clear and crisp. With a sigh of relief Harry recognised his sister's voice, and realised she must have discovered the pistol in his holster.

'Do not attempt to follow us, if you please, for I shall not hesitate to fire!'

The soldier hesitated, and eyed the slim form speculatively. An elegant silver-mounted pistol was in her grasp and it was clear by the threatening way in which it was pointed directly at the soldier's nose that she would not scruple to put her words into operation. Impotently the soldier watched as the young man struggled with his burden, finally succeeding in heaving it onto the neck of the horse.

'Mount up,' he whispered urgently, seeing the soldier take a tentative step. He swung himself into the saddle, gave a quick glance to ensure his sister was doing the same, and with an arm laid across Sir Hugh's still form heaved the animal about.

'You'll pay for this, I warrant!' shouted the soldier angrily as the two rode off with Rosamund leading Sir Hugh's horse by the reins.

'For the lord's sake, keep up!' cried Harry as he urged his laden mount through a dense clump of prickly bushes. 'That officer will wait for nought!'

'Take care of yourself, Harry!' retorted his sister from just behind. 'It was not I, you know, who instigated this mess!'

'Well, of all the ungrateful women in the world you must be the worst!' exclaimed Harry, nettled. 'It was you, my dear sister, who begged to be allowed to accompany us!'

'Yes,' she agreed calmly, 'and what a good thing it was, too! If I had not been there poor Sir Hugh would have been well on his way to Upavon, and you with him I dare swear!'

'Ha! I was never in trouble!'

'Were you not? And if I had not returned with your pistol?'

'That reminds me, thank you! Have you got it there? I shouldn't like to lose it, it's one of a pair.'

Impatiently Rosamund held out the weapon which Harry accepted and pocketed gratefully. 'Well,' he conceded, grinning in the darkness, 'I should have been in a fix if you had not appeared. There! Are you now content?'

'I shall be, if Sir Hugh is not badly hurt.'

Harry glanced down at the form bouncing just before him and said: 'We had better stop, I suppose, but not yet. I'll say this, Ros, he has a lot more to him that I thought. There was no way I could leave him behind.'

'No, I'm glad.'

They rode on for a while in silence, occasionally dropping to a walk when traversing uneven territory, but generally proceeding at a steady canter. At last Harry seemed to consider them safe for he reined in and wheeled around to face his sister.

'I think we had better stop,' he said shortly. 'Sir Hugh seems to be breathing badly. We ought to look.'

With a little difficulty Rosamund brought the two horses to a standstill, and kicked her feet free of the rough iron stirrups. Anxiously she approached her brother who had dismounted and was engaged in dragging the inanimate Sir Hugh onto the ground.

'This is hopeless, Harry,' she said, bending down over the body. 'How can we tell what is wrong when we can't see?'

'Give me your hand. He has had a bad knock here.'

Under Harry's guidance Rosamund detected the lump that had risen beneath Sir Hugh's hair, and felt on her fingers the warm stickiness of blood. She opened her mouth to speak, but at that moment there came a distinct rumble on the road beside them. She looked up sharply at her brother, and then said: 'Stop the chaise, Harry, they can take us to town!'

There was a moment's silence, and then Harry replied, his voice pregnant with mischief: 'Very well, dear Ros,' and sprang up towards the road.

'Harry!' screamed his sister after him, 'take your mask off first!' There was no reply, and it was too dark for her to see her brother's action, but she hastily pulled her own mask free of her head and stuffed it in her pocket.

Down by the road Harry was deliberating on how to stop the rapidly approaching vehicle. His inclination was to waylay it with a loud 'Halt or I fire', but at the last minute he ripped off his mask and shouted: 'Stop, if you please!' waving his arms frantically in the hope that he might just be seen in the moonlight.

Inside the chaise a tall slender figure sat shrouded in a blanket. At the sound of the cry she leant forward a little and peered from the window in time to see the coach flash past a frantically waving figure on the roadside. She frowned for a second, and then tapped smartly on the roof with the handle of her umbrella. The coachman heard the signal with amazement. He had seen the slight figure soon enough, and had immediately whipped his horses the faster, certain that the figure could only mean trouble. And now here was her Grace banging on the roof, apparently unaware of the dangers to which she could so easily be exposed by this strange and impetuous action. He reined in his team obediently, but signalled quickly to the groom to be ready with the blunderbuss, while he himself stealthily drew the stout firearm he usually kept hidden in the voluminous folds of his greatcoat.

A little out of breath Harry came running to the chaise and peered eagerly in at the window. The dim light allowed him to distinguish a form before him and he said pantingly: 'Thank you, sir! My companions and I had been attacked by footpads and one of our number is sorely injured! If I might request carriage to the next town?'

'Naturally you may,' came a soft voice in the darkness. 'James, turn about, if you please. My coachman will assist you, sir, in the carrying of your friend.'

'Thank you, ma'am! My uncle is no light-weight, and my brother, who waits with him, is little more than a boy.' He disappeared from view on the words, and in a moment the carriage began backing and turning in the road.

His mind alive with suspicion the coachman reined in once more and descended sullenly to the road. Of course, there was no accounting for the Quality, and even if her Grace had taken a maggot into her brain it was his duty merely to obey orders, but when it came to lifting suspicious persons bodily into her Grace's carriage he felt as near to leaving her service as he had done for twenty-two years. There was no objection that even he could make, however, about the young man in question when it actually came to carrying the wounded gentleman to the chaise. There was no denying the young man's standing, and he was forced to admit, albeit reluctantly, that perhaps her Grace's judgement had not been at fault.

Conveying the inanimate Sir Hugh into the carriage was no easy task. He was a tall man, and broad, and it was not without much panting and heaving that Harry and the coachman finally got him stowed. The lady, who had descended from the coach to facilitate Sir Hugh's entry, now climbed back in and seated herself opposite the still form.

'Attend to your horses, sir,' she said to Harry. 'I will see your uncle is comfortable.'

For a moment Harry hesitated, then he nodded sharply and moved away. The door stood open and at that moment the moon, which had remained hidden for some little time, came from behind a cloud and fell full into the carriage. The light it afforded was not considerable, but it was sufficient for her to see that the strip of material around the gentleman's face was, in fact, no bandage as she had at first thought, but a mask, fastened at the back with two thin strings. Frowning a little the lady somewhat hastily slipped the mask from over Sir Hugh's eyes, and stared down into features almost as familiar as her own.

With a start she became aware of a shadow in the doorway, and turned to look into a very youthful face that was turned up to her with an expression of anxiety.

'Do you think he will be all right, ma'am?' asked the boy in a curiously gruff voice.

The Dowager Duchess of Ashborne hesitated. There was something peculiar about the whole affair, but the face illuminated by the fading light of the moon was open and innocent and she smiled down into it. 'I believe you need not worry,' she said. 'It is merely a graze, little more. I expect your uncle will wake up shortly with little more than a severe headache.'

'Oh, I pray you might be right,' exclaimed the youth, climbing into the carriage and perching on the edge of the seat at the dowager's invitation. 'We were waylaid, you know, and my uncle tried to fight off the villains!'

The Duchess's eyes twinkled but she said seriously: 'Good heavens! How very brave of him! Were you hurt at all?'

167

The youth shook his head vigorously. 'And we didn't lose our money either! My brother Harry chased them off!'

'Indeed! These footpads seem to have taken on more than they bargained for!'

'Yes!' agreed Rosamund with a funny little squeak to her voice as she thought of the unfortunate soldiers they had left sprawled on the road. 'Oh, here is Harry! Harry,' she said, as the Viscount climbed into the carriage, 'I have just been telling this kind lady how brave you and Uncle Jasper were to scare away those dreadful footpads!'

'Really, George,' said Harry, seating himself in the corner, 'you must not bore our kind hostess with those tales. Pray forgive him, ma'am, he is but young.'

'As a matter of fact I was very interested,' said her Grace, banging on the roof again with her umbrella. 'There are far too many of these fellows on the roads. I am truly sorry you were not able to take them captive.'

'Well, we could have done,' responded Rosamund, warming to her role, 'but Harry would have it that Uncle Jasper was more important so we had to let them escape.'

'I am sure Harry was right,' said her Grace gravely, thankful that the chaise was too dark for them to see the smile on her lips. 'But I am extremely curious to know why you were out so late. It is surely past midnight.'

'It is,' Rosamund blithely agreed, 'but Harry was so anxious to see the cockfight at Bulford today, though why I can't conceive because I thought it merely unpleasant.'

'Well, you shouldn't have insisted on going, then, should you,' retorted Harry with a glare at his supposed brother. 'You really are an ungrateful young cub!'

'At least I didn't lose my shilling,' countered Rosamund, ruthlessly sacrificing her brother's reputation.

Since it seemed likely that the brothers would come to blows if the conversation continued on these lines the Duchess hastily intervened, saying: 'Very praiseworthy, George! Now tell me, sir, where you wish me to put you down.'

The question successfully silenced them. Harry glanced uncertainly at his twin, then said: 'We are journeying back to Andover, ma'am. If you could convey us thither we will be able to take care of my uncle.'

'Certainly,' responded her Grace, at once. 'If you will give me your direction I will order my coachman there.'

'We're putting up at an inn,' said Rosamund, promptly, 'so there is no need for you to take us all the way there. Harry and your strong coachman can easily put Uncle Jasper back on his horse.'

'And how, I wonder, will the inn greet your arrival with a wounded man in the small hours of the morning?'

'I beg you not to trouble yourself, ma'am,' said Harry, quickly. 'You have been too kind already.'

'Nonsense,' replied her Grace, briskly. 'Naturally we shall convey you to the inn. Which is it?'

Harry stared. For perhaps the first time in his life his mind was a blank. He had not done more than pass through Andover in his life, and he had no idea what inn it contained. 'The George,' he said firmly, hoping his hesitation did not betray the uncertainty he felt.

'Ah, the George, an excellent inn!' responded her Grace immediately. 'I never put up anywhere else myself.' She banged smartly on the roof and when the coachman reined in to desire her pleasure she ordered him to take them to the George Inn at Andover.

'The George, your Grace? It was burned down six months ago, your Grace!'

'Thank you, John. You may drive on.'

There was a brief silence, and then the coach lurched forward again and the Duchess leant back against the squabs.

'You must think it very odd, ma'am,' said Harry after a moment's hesitation, 'but I do believe I mistook the name! It was of course the George we stayed at last year!'

Slowly the Duchess turned her head to regard him coolly. 'And where are you staying this year?'

'At the other one!' responded Rosamund at once.

'How stupid of me!' exclaimed her Grace with a little exclamation. 'You are of course staying at the Angel, naturally you are.'

There came two almost audible sighs of relief, and Harry relaxed against the squabs. They continued in silence for another minute or so, then the Duchess said: 'I am really very unfair to you, indeed, but you have been such foolish children.' She gave a little laugh and regarded them in the dim light of the chaise. 'I fear there is no Angel at Andover! But it was wicked of me to lead you on like that, but indeed I could not resist!' She took a breath, then said more seriously. 'I must tell you that I am the Duchess of Ashbourne and I have been acquainted with Hugh Eavleigh these twenty years.'

There was a stunned silence. The carriage clattered noisily over a rough section of road but the twins sat still, hearing nothing but the pounding of their own hearts.

'What do you intend to do, your Grace?' Rosamund asked at last.

The lady smiled. 'As to that I am not sure. At first I was going to hand you over to the magistrates, for I was certain you must be abducting poor Hugh! Then it began to seem most odd that you should choose my carriage for such a venture, particularly when you had three good horses of your own. And then, you know, you do not behave like common criminals. What puzzled me most, however, was the fact that poor Hugh was actually wearing a mask, like a veritable highwayman! So now I have come to the conclusion that whatever nefarious business you two are up to Hugh is as involved as you are, in which case I am resolved to help you in any way I can. Do you care to tell me?'

The tale which then tumbled out was extraordinary. It was with a little hesitation that Rosamund revealed her sex and her identity but the Duchess gave no indication that she found Rosamund's necessity to disguise herself as a boy to recover the emerald as extraordinary. Little was omitted. Her Grace proved to be a sympathetic listener, accepting without question Harry's means of amusing himself, and even going so far as to say she often felt like defying convention herself.

'So you see,' concluded Rosamund, 'we really had to do something about poor Sir Hugh, especially after he had been good enough to concern himself in our affairs.'

The Duchess chuckled. 'Poor Hugh! How surprised he must have been to find himself masked and attacking soldiers, all for the purpose of recovering a ring!'

'But if I do not recover it, your Grace,' Harry said, 'I shall be in a devil of a fix!'

'You cannot simply tell the Earl that you have lost it?'

'He would never accept such a tale! He knows how glad I was to receive it, and that I should never let it out of my sight. Besides, it was devilish tight. There's no way it could have come off by chance. In fact, that fellow, Dick nearly took my finger with it!'

'And I suppose,' ventured the Duchess tentatively, 'that it is too much to ask you simply to tell your father what happened?'

'I fear so, your Grace,' replied Rosamund, before her brother could make the crushing retort that sprang to his lips.

Her Grace nodded. 'I feared as much. Just what do you intend to do now?'

The twins looked at each other. 'We haven't decided,' Rosamund said at last. 'I suppose they will take Dick to the Justice and the lock-up. I have no doubt either but that Harry will devise some method of recovery for the ring.'

'But naturally,' concurred the Duchess, frowning a little. 'It seems to me, my dears,' she said at last, 'that you cannot return to your estimable parent with this tale, nor can you take my poor friend to a common inn. I have decided, therefore, to conduct you to Ashbourne Park where you will be my guests. I think it will be wisest, you know, and we may concoct a letter to your harassed father assuring him that you have not, after all, eloped, but have decided to accept a pressing invitation from your dear friend, her Grace of Ashbourne — how well that sounds! — in order to escape temporarily the pressures of Daviot. And you, you hopeless boy, will also write to your father informing him of your decision to stay over for a few days at Ashbourne, thus avoiding any possibility of his lordship's discovering your loss.' She paused, and peered hopefully at the two dim figures beside her.

For several seconds there was total silence, then Rosamund said, meditatively: 'I feel I should say something like: 'We have trespassed overmuch on your Grace already', but I fear I never was one for the social niceties! Do you really think you can put up with such a harum-scarum pair as us?'

The Duchess laughed. 'My dear! You have simply no idea how bored I become in the country! These evening parties are so dull! Indeed, if you do not come freely, I believe I shall be forced to abduct you.'

9

Ashbourne Park was a large and stately mansion of Tudor construction occupying a full valley of its own and completely hidden from inquisitive eyes by a surrounding wall of woods. The present incumbent was a carefree gentleman of thirty, who was content to let his Mama reside in his house and run his servants, which she did to perfection. He had acceded some seven years previously, and from the first had been disposed to let his Mama rule his household. He had little thought for such affairs, and she had been doing it so admirably for so many years that he saw or reason why she should not continue. The Duchess, meanwhile, was perfectly content with this state of affairs. She loved her son, but she was not possessive, and indeed it worried her occasionally that the Duke should not take more than the most passing of interests in the fairer sex. Indeed, when the time came she fully intended to retire gracefuly to her own establishment among her friends and have no more say in the running of Ashbourne than if she had never reigned there. For the moment, however, she was content with her lot. Her son came and went as often as he pleased, was singularly undemanding in his requirements, and if his mother just happened to be present when he arrived with a party of friends, so much the better.

The decision made — and indeed it was a difficult one for nobody — the three passed the rest of the short journey in attendance on Sir Hugh, who had groaned impressively, thus attracting attention to himself. Rosamund, in fact, felt rather guilty to have paid so little attention to her wounded gallant, and beguiled the next few minutes in peering studiously at his ashen countenance. After the groan that had reminded the party of their duty he had not stirred again, and Rosamund felt a tremor in her heart as she considered what might be amiss.

The Duchess was apparently expected. Lights were to be seen in several chambers, and as the carriage rolled smoothly to the entrance the door opened, revealing an aged and portly individual bearing a branch of candles in one hand.

'Good evening, your Grace,' he said, bowing as low as his rotundity would allow, 'a pleasant evening, I trust?'

'Thank you, Hammet, very pleasant. Will you ask Mrs. Filde to prepare three bedchambers, please. I have brought guests with me.'

If Hammet found it extraordinary that her Grace, having spent the evening at a whist party with some very old friends, should return in the small hours with three strangers he gave no sign of it, merely bowing, and reflecting inwardly that if her Grace chose to act in such a way there was doubtless an excellent reason behind it all. Mrs. Filde's opinions were, however, rather more volubly voiced, but since only one other chamber maid was privileged to hear them the effect upon her Grace might be said to have been minimal. One of the younger footmen, summoned with a colleague to bear the inanimate Sir Hugh upstairs, was indeed sufficiently unprepared for this eventuality to give a look of surprise, but Hammet, observing this lapse, quelled him with an icy stare, and he thereafter dedicated himself to the execution of his duties.

The physician, summoned at a dreaded hour by the garbled tale of a domestic was in no good humour when finally he arrived at Ashbourne Park. One glance had satisfied her Grace that they could not wait until morning, and accordingly she had wasted no time, having regard neither for her own rest nor for that of her doctor. Once inside the bed-chamber, however, Dr. Supple's professional pride overtook him and he went about his business with much humming and ha'ing, all of which served to cast Rosamund into greater anxiety. The verdict, however, was not unpropitious. To be sure, the gentleman had been unconscious rather long, but this was not unusual, and Dr. Supple saw little to worry him in the actual nature of the wound. He left a cordial to be administered as soon as the patient wakened, and promised to call back on the following day. Attempts by the ladies to draw a more hopeful opinion from him failed, and he merely waggled a finger at them and told them not to be impatient.

★ ★ ★

Sir Hugh lay perfectly still and told himself not to get anxious. The fact that the last thing he could remember was being bound by a soldier was not propitious, but he had to admit that the velvet hangings about the bed were not what one usually associated with lock-ups. For some reason he felt curiously light-headed. He knew no urge to sit up and discover his whereabouts, but was perfectly content to lie on his back and stare at the hangings above him. Indeed, it was all very strange. He wondered vaguely what had become of the twins, but even this did not stir him overmuch. He sighed contentedly and wriggled his toes beneath the covers.

There was an immediate response. An exclamation came from somewhere beside his left ear, and he was aware of feet crossing a thickly carpeted floor, then of a door opening and closing softly. He attempted to bend his mind to consideration of this event, but his brain was unusually dull, and refused to co-operate. He decided to set it from him, and closed his eyes again.

When next he opened his eyes the daylight had faded. The hangings above him were no longer discernible, and he was aware of a thin shaft of light that pierced the darkness on his left. He felt rather better now than he had done, and aroused himself sufficiently to turn his head on the pillow. As he did so he was aware of a curious awkwardness. His head felt several times larger than usual, but surely this could not be, and he dismissed it, concentrating instead on his new field of vision. This included a chair. Seated in it was a female he had no recollection of having seen before, but the white lace cap told him she was a maid of some sort, probably one of a more superior breed, since kitchen domestics did not wear lace. A solitary candle stood on a narrow chest beside her, casting its inadequate light on an expanse of white material draped over her knees, and which she appeared to be in some way of mending. He decided inconsequentially that she presented a decidedly restful picture, and wondered why his own servants were never as pretty. Suddenly she seemed to become aware of his regard for she raised her head and forced her lips into a soundless 'O'.

'Sir!' she exclaimed, in a soft musical voice. 'Are you well?' She stood up, and carefully folded the sheet. 'How is your head? Shall I fetch her Grace?'

No lock-up, then. 'Thank you,' said a man's voice, then he realised it was his own, curiously detached and unfamiliar. He felt an absurd desire to laugh, but repressed it, and watched as the girl crossed the room quickly.

Left alone again Sir Hugh resumed his contemplation of the dim ceiling, drifting in and out of slumber until a sharp click recalled him and with an effort he strained his eyes towards the door. A tall slim woman was approaching, blonde hair shot occasionally with silver swept up and back from her face, high cheek bones, delicate nostrils, firm, curved lips. He frowned for a moment in an effort of concentration, then his brow cleared.

'Good God!' he said faintly. 'Katie!'

The lady smiled, and approached his bedside. 'Hello, Hugh,' she said, bending over him. 'How is the head?'

'It feels fine. Is there something wrong with it?'

'You had a knock, that's all. You should be on your feet again in a couple of days.'

'A couple of days?' he ejaculated, attempting to sit up. He gave a groan, and dropped back onto the pillows. 'Well, perhaps you might be right. What happened?'

The Duchess's lips twitched. 'I gather, Hugh, dear, that you had a disagreement with a soldier.'

'Lord, yes! I say, Katie, have you come across a couple of ragamuffins name of Daviot?'

She smiled and seated herself in the chair abandoned by the maid. 'Don't worry about them, Hugh. They are here. In fact, it is them you have to thank. They saved you, you know, and hailed me into the bargain. You are at Ashbourne.'

Sir Hugh's eyes flickered. 'Am I, indeed! Is Stephen here?'

She shook her head. 'Lincolnshire,

for a few days, which is perhaps a little fortunate, though it is not likely he would mind, knowing Stephen. However, it allows me a free hand. I should not like him even to *think* disapprovingly of me!'

'I doubt if it would even cross his mind,' opined Hugh, his eyes twinkling at her. 'But those young rascals of mine, you say they are well?'

'In health *and* spirits, Hugh, dear. That foolish boy is planning a number of extraordinarily feckless schemes for the recovery of his wretched ring!'

Sir Hugh's eyes widened appreciatively. 'So you know about that! I'm surprised, I must admit, but I suppose there are few who can resist your charms!'

'Tush!' said her Grace roundly. 'Charm had nothing to do with it. They were imprisoned in my carriage with an injured man to boot! No story would suffice.'

'I daresay not, but I must admit I'm amazed that you believed it, such a tale as it is!'

She smiled kindly down at him. 'A tale indeed! But that ring is an heirloom, you know. I can see no way around it. He must get it back.'

'Of course he must, but I wish you would let me see him before he does anything reckless!' Sir Hugh struggled to sit up, but the Duchess, calm and authoritative, gently pressed him back into the pile of pillows. 'You may see Rosamund, perhaps, in the morning, but not Harry. Dr. Supple says you are not to be excited.'

'May I not see her now? I feel not the least bit tired!'

'I daresay you do not, but what of the rest of us? It may have escaped your notice, Hugh, dear, but it is after half past three! Your ragamuffin Rosamund has been in bed these four hours!'

Sir Hugh groaned. 'Lord! How long have I been here?'

'Twenty-four hours, or so.'

He blinked at her. 'And I was unconscious all that time?'

She nodded. 'It was a bad knock,

you know. At one point you had us quite worried!'

He chuckled and relaxed. 'Very well, Katie, but promise me you will not let that cub do anything foolish! I feel, the lord knows why, in some sort responsible for the boy.'

'The lord knows indeed! But there, I give my word.'

That seemed to calm him, for he settled down more comfortably and closed his eyes. After a minute or two he opened them, however, and fixed them upon the fair face beside him. 'I'd be obliged,' he said, smiling, 'if you would send for my valet. The poor fellow must be half-mad with worry.'

'Do not concern yourself, Hugh, dear. Steering was collected from the Bull this morning, and is here with all your clothes. Now do get some rest!'

Deciding that it was really very comforting to be treated masterfully on occasion, Sir Hugh shut his eyes with a smile and drifted back into untroubled slumber.

The news that Sir Hugh had apparently recovered from his accident was greeted generally with relief.

'You know, Ros,' said Harry, waving his fork at her across the breakfast table the next morning. 'I think if something had happened to poor old Eavleigh I would have had little heart to continue, I swear I would!'

Rosamund smiled, but said: 'Indeed, Harry, I wish you would tell me what you had in mind.'

'How can I, sister dear, when I don't know myself!'

'You say that, but you forget how well I know you! You've had a plan ever since you failed last night, I know it.'

His eyes twinkled at her. 'Then, my dear Ros, there is no need for me to tell you, is there?'

Rosamund made an exasperated gesture. 'I wish you were not so careless about this business, indeed I do! We are no longer at home, remember. What will the Duchess say to your gallivanting?'

'Her Grace is a supporter of mine,' said Harry, carelessly spearing a second slice of beef onto the end of his knife. 'I daresay she will think it a very good lark if I succeed in bringing home the ring.'

'She might, I suppose, but I doubt if she would appreciate it overmuch if she finds herself embroiled with a gallows-bird!'

Harry grimaced. 'You forget my sensibilities, sweet sister! I've no intention of ending on the nubbing-cheat!'

'Of course you have not, but has it escaped your notice that Huffy White was hanged last month at Leeds?'

He smiled now. 'No, dear Ros, I saw the report. Did you not notice what he said when asked if there was anything that would comfort him? 'All I want is some other man to hang in my stead'! Indeed, Ros, I would feign go that way.'

Rosamund made an impatient gesture. 'If that is your attitude I must have done with you. There is no reasoning!'

His smile faded and he eyed her thoughtfully for a moment. 'What is it, fair Rosamund?' he asked at last. 'You were never wont to be so stuffy, indeed! Are you ill?'

'No, not ill, but worried for you, Harry. This is no longer a game, and you don't seem to realise!'

'I don't see the difference between this and what we did before, certainly. Indeed, I would have thought you would find my resolve more praise-worthy. At least I have some object in mind!'

Rosamund attempted a smile. 'How disobliging I am, to be sure! It is just I am so certain you will be captured if you try anything else! Will you not let the ring go?'

Now he was truly astonished. 'What are you at, child, in even speaking thus? Has my staid friend Hugh been influencing you?'

She gave an unsteady laugh. 'I think he has! So brave as he was, and so disapproving! I thought, Harry, that he was affecting you as well.'

'Well, you're out there,' he answered shortly, throwing down his napkin. 'The ring is mine and I do not mean to lose it. You will not dissuade me, you know, so I wish you would not try.'

Rosamund, looking up at his handsome, drawn face, decided that he was in earnest, and stifled a small sigh. Seeing that she had no more to say Harry scraped back his chair and left the room.

Rosamund did not see him again that day. Immediately after leaving her Harry sought out their hostess, requested her to send a servant for their clothes, handed over a brief note to his father, and absented himself. He was going, he told her plainly, to recover his ring, and he would be very grateful if she would say nothing to his sister. All this was very politely worded and the Duchess, by no means impervious to the young man's careless charm, agreed to do as he bade her, although she did mention that Sir Hugh had asked to see him before he left on any dare-devil missions.

At this Harry grinned. 'I daresay, ma'am, but what will he say to me? Merely that I am foolish and reckless, which I know already, and that I would be far better advised to forget the wretched thing. Well, your Grace, I can't do that, though doubtless the advice is sound enough, so I prefer to present him with a 'fait accompli'. He is a good fellow, I admire him, but would it not be inadvisable to worry him just now?'

The Duchess smiled. 'I won't tell him, if that's what you want, but I must ask you to take care! My groom, Jameson, is a trustworthy fellow, you know. I daresay he would hold your horse to perfection!'

'Thank you! But do you think he would appreciate being sent to wait on a potential gallows-bird like me? I shall do well enough, I believe, as long as I know you are not all worrying about me.'

'And if you don't return?'

He shrugged. 'I shall contrive, I don't doubt. You might ask a servant to wait up, perhaps. At all costs, do not let Rosamund ride out for me. She has too much nerve for comfort!'

'That I can believe! Very well, my lord, I will do as you ask, since I have no control over you, but you will not censure me, I trust, if I ask you to take care?'

His eyes twinkled at her. 'Keep my Rosamund safe, Duchess. With luck I shall be back before I'm missed. Good day!'

As it happened Rosamund did not need to be told. She was too familiar with her twin to be taken in by the Duchess's story that Kearsley had gone with the servant for their clothes so that he might speak with their father, and the Duchess realised by the sharp look in Rosamund's eyes that the tale had fallen wide of the mark.

'He has gone to Upavon, has he not? I know him too well, you see. I could tell this morning he was planning something, but he won't let me help him. If only I could make him understand how much I worry for him!'

The Duchess hesitated and then said: 'I believe he will be safe enough. He is no fool, your brother, I am sure, and I don't doubt that when he has his ring he will be content. Try not to worry.'

Rosamund smiled and nodded, and after a moment asked casually if she might visit Sir Hugh.

It was obvious to this gentleman, when she entered his room a little later, that all was not well with her. He smiled and held out his hand, and as she took it and sat down beside him he said, a shade sharply: 'What is it? Why are you concerned?'

She attempted a laugh and said lightly: 'Oh, 'tis nothing, indeed! Merely my noisome brother, but I daresay it is all well. He is not stupid, after all!'

She laughed again, but Sir Hugh, eyeing her keenly, was not deceived, and said quickly: 'Where is the fellow? Let me talk to him.'

She hesitated, then meeting his intense gaze said frankly: 'He has already gone. The Duchess says it is to collect our clothes and tell Papa but I know it is not, and I cannot but worry.'

Sir Hugh swore softly and said: 'Indeed, I had not thought her so little to be trusted! I asked so particularly that she should send him to me before she let him leave!'

'Do not blame her,' Rosamund said quickly. 'You do not know how adept Harry is at persuading people, ladies particularly, I'm afraid! And I don't doubt he told her it would be best not to worry you, either, so really it is as much your fault as hers!'

He laughed then, and relieved Rosamund greatly, who had been concerned at how grey and tense he was looking. The laugh died, however, and the eyes, heavy and shadowed, turned back to her with every appearance of anxiety. 'If only I weren't laid by the heels!' he exclaimed, stirring restlessly beneath the covers. 'I feel so helpless, and all that cursed medic can say is that I must lie quietly and rest, and give me some foul liquid to drink! Indeed, it is enough to make a man turn to Blue Ruin!'

Rosamund gave a shaky laugh, for she was startled by the sudden wild look in Sir Hugh's usually quiet eyes. He saw her expression, and, relaxing again, smiled up at her. 'Don't worry, I don't mean it! I've had my chance for that sort of foolery, and if I didn't indulge in my mad youth I'm unlikely to now!'

Rosamund gave him an odd look and seemed about to say something, but then apparently changed her mind.

'I want you to promise me, Rose,' said Hugh, when it became obvious she was not going to speak, 'do not go after that young rogue. I cannot do with two of you in the lock-up!'

She noted the concern in his eyes and said quickly: 'Don't worry, I shall not! I have to admit, however, that I shall find it very difficult to stay still until I know what he is about! As long as I am with him I am quite easy, but as soon as he is on his own I never know what he might do!'

Viscount Kearsley, riding sedately towards Upavon, was undecided as to his course of action. There was no way in which his restless mind would let him abide inactivity at Ashbourne, and he was glad simply to be out of the house. So far, his plan extended to riding out to Upavon, where he would observe the setting, and, if possible, make plans for his jewel's recovery. Dick, he knew, would be in the lock-up attached to Justice Kingman's home, and he felt it would not be a difficult task to isolate this one part of the building from the rest, attended as it would be by at least one gaoler. It seemed likely that Dick would have been brought before the Justice the day before, and he was therefore anxious to recover his jewel before Dick could be sent to the sessions at Salisbury. A slight problem existed in discovering the whereabouts of the ring, for it was certain that the gaolers would have removed it along with the other property, and would have handed it to Sir Joshua for safety. Mulling this over as he rode Harry decided that his best course of action would be to release the highwayman and enlist his support in discovering the whereabouts of the emerald.

It was a dubious plan, and one that involved considerable dependence on the highwayman's sense of gratitude. The various repercussions that might ensue from the plan's misfiring were unpleasant, and Harry preferred not to dwell overlong on these.

It was about ten miles from Appleshaw to Upavon, and since Harry did not hurry he did not arrive until late afternoon. He stopped off on the way for a tankard of bad ale and something to eat, and spent over two hours in the coffee room of the inn attempting to consolidate his plans. By the time he arrived at Upavon these can only be described as being of the loosest, and he determined, as usual, to rely on his instincts, and his customary good luck.

The house was not difficult to find, a large, square-faced building fronting the road, a quadrangle with inner courtyard gained through a high archway set into the front of the mansion. Harry had long since determined that the lock-up must be through this archway, and accordingly took up a position on a vantage point some hundred yards away from the building. A small clump of trees and bushes surrounded the little hump, and, tethering Sally carefully to one low-sweeping branch, he lay down flat on his stomach to observe the movements of the house's occupants.

Not a patient gentleman, by the time he had lain two hours on the hard uneven earth he felt sufficiently conversant with the building to put his plan into operation. He had not intended to do more than observe, but now that he was there it seemed a shame not to take advantage of the situation. At first there had been considerable traffic in and out of the courtyard, carriages, dog-carts, solitary riders and walkers. For the last half hour, however, nothing had either entered or left, and he was beginning to hope that the business of the day might now be concluded. He had no difficulty in deciding that the tall, grey-haired gentleman saying goodbye to the solitary gentleman on horseback had been Sir Joshua, and although he would infinitely have preferred him to be from home he anticipated no difficulty. Now that it was finally growing dark, therefore, he decided it was time he made a move.

Tied on to the back of his saddle, and screwed tightly into a bundle, was the large, heavy greatcoat Harry kept for operations such as these. He pulled it out now, and having divested himself of his elegant riding jacket he shrugged the heavy coat onto his shoulders and pulled it up around his chin. It threatened to make him unsufferably hot, but he did not anticipate staying long within the precincts of the house, and tried to ignore the great weight about his shoulders. His topboots gleamed from beneath its folds but he seemed not to care, merely pulling from his pocket the black cloth mask that would cover his face from his nose to his eyebrows. Although he intended being seen by nobody he did not wish to run the risk of ending his days on the gallows with Dick.

By the time he set off the sun was down and the front of the house deeply cast in shadow. There was still sufficient daylight left for him to see by, however, and Harry hoped to be well away by the time night had fallen.

As he moved slowly towards the house in the cover of a line of trees sounds of activity came from within the courtyard. He could plainly hear a horse being led across the cobbles, and as he strained his ears he caught the muffled sounds of conversation. Impetuously Harry left the cover of the trees and walked boldly across the long grass to the corner of the archway. Peering round, he looked into the yard and saw a horse being led by the reins through a corresponding archway on the opposite side. A few seconds later a door somewhere opened and closed, and the yard fell silent. Deftly Harry pulled up the mask he had looped around his neck so that it effectively concealed his identity. As he moved under the archway he felt the customary excitement welling in his breast and chuckled softly to himself. If only Ros were there!

As he had thought, the courtyard was now deserted. All round him were doors and low archways leading mysteriously into dark passages or up stairs, and for a moment he hesitated in indecision.

Then there came the unmistakable sound of a heavy door opening, and footsteps echoed from down one of the dim passages. In a moment a man appeared. Harry, under the protection of the archway, could see him dimly. He was a broad fellow, dressed in buff breeches and jerkin, and carrying a tray on which reposed a couple of empty plates and a tankard. A small bundle of keys depended from his belt on a string. Crossing the court diagonally he made his way slowly to a low wooden door, and in a couple of moments had disappeared behind it.

Having waited a minute or so longer to make sure the fellow was not returning Harry crept from the cover of the arch and ran, without looking round, for the arch through which the gaoler had come. It led onto a narrow passage which almost immediately went into a corner, and then, beyond this, into a flight of very steep stone steps. At the bottom of those Harry hesitated and peered upwards speculatively but it was almost totally dark and the stairs disappeared without giving any indication of where they were going. Harry was not one to lack spirit, however, and trod resolutely up the stairway, one hand on the rough stone wall to guide himself.

The reason for the darkness was almost immediately apparent. He had mounted barely half a dozen steps before the wall gave out beneath his fingers and he discovered the stairway to turn at right angles to itself. At the top he could now perceive the faintest glimmer of light, and he resolutely ascended the remaining stairs.

The stairs gave onto an uncarpeted passage stretching away in front of him and to the left. At the far end before him was a long window through which the last of the daylight was filtering, showing to him a number of doors on either side of the corridor. He hesitated for a moment, then approached the first of these and peered through the narrow barred window that was set into the stout wood. It was the first view Harry had had of a cell, and its dim condition did nothing to endear it to him. He could make out very little, but the slight movement of something on the straw encouraged him to whisper sharply: 'Dick! Are you in there?'

For a second there was total silence, then a voice, pregnant with suspicion, snapped out: 'Who's that?'

They got no further. From the stairway came the gaoler bearing a tray with a bowl of food. For a second he failed to see the figure in the large greatcoat, then he stopped sharply. 'What d'you think you're doing?' he demanded, starting forward.

Harry sprung round, and confronted the fellow as he approached, still bearing the tray. With a curse he sprang forward, plunging his hand into the deep pocket that contained his pistol. Seeing this motion the gaoler cast aside the tray, sending the bowl and its contents flying, and grabbed the heavy cudgel that was pushed under his belt. With a growl he started forward just as Harry, who had had difficulty in extricating his weapon, succeeded in freeing it from the folds of his coat and levelling it at the approaching man. Behind the black mask his eyes glittered dangerously, and he carefully pulled the trigger.

It was with a chill of horror that he heard the hammer click down and realised the pistol was empty. He turned the weapon swiftly in his hand, intending to use it as a club, but the gaoler was already on top of him, his arm raised threateningly above his head. It descended sharply and crunched sickeningly into the base of Harry's neck, causing him to reel drunkenly into the rough stone wall. His vision blurred he lunged desperately and had the satisfaction of seeing, albeit indistinctly, his assailant crumple at his feet. Instinct now took over, and he half ran half staggered to the top of the stairs, the blow he had received threatening every minute to overwhelm him. He had just put his foot to the first stair when the unmistakable sound of boots on stone reached him from just below. He turned at once, carefully cradling his rapidly stiffening left arm and staggered down the other passage. A few seconds later he heard an exclamation and forced himself into a run. Dots were now leaping before his eyes, and the passage seemed to be growing gradually steeper. Of a sudden he encountered a solid wall, and reeled for a second before discovering the passage to proceed at right angles. It finished with a door, large and impressively studded and braced. It yielded to his pressure and he almost fell through it onto the now thickly carpeted floor. Steadying himself on the wall he peered forward drunkenly, and after a second realised he was in some sort of gallery, hung on both sides with family portraits. He gradually became aware of pounding footsteps behind him and forced himself to move on. The gallery was flanked on one side by a number of doors, and at the far end was a pair of doors. He closed his eyes for a second, and then fixed them with great determination on the doors ahead. As he lunged towards them however, sounds came from the other side, and with a kind of fascination he watched as the handle turned with maddening slowness. At once his retreating senses grew distinct. He spun on his heel and headed for the first door before him, one of several that opened from the wall on his right. The door opened easily and he had staggered through and closed it before he realised the room was not empty. With an effort he made a bow.

'Forgive me, ma'am, for the intrusion. I — ' and then the darkness that had been drawing ever nearer suddenly crept up and received him.

10

The girl had been seated in the window embrasure, a square of embroidery spread on her lap, but now she leapt up and started forward in consternation. At the sound of Harry's fall a tall spare female in middle age had come from the adjoining chamber, and now the young lady turned to her. 'Lock the door, Davey, quickly!'

'What are you about, Miss Cressy?' the woman demanded, her voice pregnant with suspicion.

Her mistress turned imploring eyes upon her. 'Oh Davey, please, do not fail me!'

Miss Davidson sniffed, but nevertheless locked the door, and turned again to her mistress, bent over the crumpled form. 'He is ill,' she pronounced at last. 'Help me get him to my bed.'

'Now, Miss Cressy, what do you

think you're about?'

'Help me, please, or I shall hurt myself!' Since she already had her hands beneath the gentleman's shoulders Miss Davidson judged it best to comply, and she had just raised his legs when the sound of commotion came from outside. 'Do hurry, Davey!' hissed the girl, urgently, blue eyes imploring.

'What man?' came a male voice, strong and vibrant, from the passage.

The reply was muffled, but the young lady besought her maid urgently to hurry up, and between them they struggled into the adjoining bed-chamber. They had just succeeded in laying him, none too carefully, upon the bed, when a pounding came from the other room and the voice sounded again.

'Cressida! Why is your door locked? Open it at once!'

Miss Cressida Kingman cast an imploring glance at her disapproving maid, then hurried into her sitting-room to open the door.

'Why, Papa!' she exclaimed, raising one hand to her golden curls as though she had been thus engaged, 'what is the matter?'

The gentleman, tall and lean and with a strong aquiline countenance, set her gently to one side and entered the room. 'Why was your door locked, Cressida?' he demanded, casting a sweeping glance around him.

'I was just about to change for dinner, Papa.'

His eyes burned down at her, as if trying to determine some hidden truth. 'Why was your door locked?' he repeated.

She gave a little laugh. 'Papa, you do not mind, surely! Davey was with me, and you know I never feel safe when we have prisoners in the house!'

He appeared to consider this, and then, as if satisfied, nodded sharply, and turned on his heel. At the door he hesitated, and turned back. 'I wish you to lock it again after me,' he said. 'There is a fellow loose. I shouldn't want you disturbed.'

'What sort of — fellow, Papa?' Cressida inquired, looking innocently at her parent.

'Just a rascal, my dear, nothing for you to worry about. But keep your door locked.'

'Very well, Papa, if that is what you wish.'

He gave her a penetrating glance, and then nodded, and left the room. Cressida at once flew to the door and with hands that trembled violently succeeded in turning the key once more.

'What in heaven's name are you about, Miss Cressy?' inquired the maid, appearing from the bedroom.

'Oh Davey, please don't betray me! But how could I let them take the poor man away? Anyone can see he's ill!'

'Yes, and it seems to me there's a maggot in your brain, Miss Cressy! Didn't you hear your father say he was a villain?'

She nodded. 'Of course, but I don't

believe it. Didn't you hear how he addressed me before he collapsed? I'm sure he's a gentleman, and I mean to help him!'

Miss Davidson raised her eyes to heaven and followed her mistress into the bedchamber. 'What your poor mother would say I shudder to think,' she announced with all the freedom of a valued retainer. 'Gentlemen in your bedroom! Such impropriety!'

'Oh fudge,' said Cressida roundly, staring down at the still form. 'What harm can he do in this state? Oh Davey, I'm sure he's hurt!' She put out a hand as she spoke and carefully removed the black mask that had concealed all but his mouth from view. Miss Davidson sniffed.

'He's a handsome boy, at any rate,' she said, staring down at the pallid face.

'Yes, but see how pale he is! Oh Davey, do please help me! We must find out if he is hurt!' She began fumbling with his greatcoat as she spoke, but at this Miss Davidson stepped forward and quietly but firmly moved her mistress out of the way.

'Since you're determined, and I can see you are, though the Lord knows why, you'd better let me do it. It's hardly the job for a lady of your class.'

Cressida made an impatient sound, but nevertheless stood back, and watched avidly as her maid carefully removed the coat.

She was a small young lady, measuring barely five feet one inch, and had but recently celebrated her eighteenth birthday. Guinea-gold curls artlessly tumbled about a little heart-shaped face, and two enormous eyes, so dark a blue as to be almost violet, stared mischievously onto the world from beneath long dark curling lashes. She was a lovely little thing, and while at one of Bath's most select seminaries had become quite used to admiring glances when she walked out with her school-mates and teacher. Her schooling had finished some months previously, and she was now waiting eagerly for the new season which with any luck would see her in London.

'I think I shall have to help you after all,' she said now having watched for several minutes as her maid struggled with the great-coat.

Miss Davidson jumped, having assumed her mistress to have left the room, but said grudgingly: 'Take his head, Miss Cressy, and I'll ease him out of it.' They managed it at last, and it was immediately apparent to both ladies from the quality of his shirt and breeches that here was no ordinary young highwayman.

'I was right!' exclaimed Cressida, staring down at him. 'He is a gentleman, Davey, surely you see!'

'Yes,' she admitted grudgingly, 'but I'd still like to know what he was doing with that mask on his face!'

'So would I,' admitted Cressida, 'but that can wait. Can you tell if he is hurt?'

Miss Davidson sniffed, but nevertheless laid a hand on the invalid's brow. 'He hasn't a fever, at any rate,' she said shortly.

'But he's so pale! What can be the matter?'

Miss Davidson stared at him a moment longer, and then her eye caught sight of something just about the folds of his neckcloth. Deftly she removed it, and a large area, discolouring almost as they looked at it, was immediately apparent, stretching across his neck and down under his shirt. Miss Davidson hesitated no longer, but quickly ripped the shirt open and laid bare the Viscount's shoulder.

The injury was obvious. The bruising was livid, and even as Miss Davidson's practised fingers ran over the tender area she knew what was wrong. 'The bone's broken, Miss Cressy. This is no job for me.'

She spoke with studied lightness, but Cressida was quick to catch the edge of worry in her voice. 'Davey, what can we do? If I tell Papa he might be hanged!'

'Nonsense!' said Miss Davidson roundly, but even as she said it she felt a chill at her heart as she looked at the pale handsome face. She frowned down at him for several minutes, always conscious of the fidgeting figure at her side, desperately trying to find a solution compatible with the propriety of the affair and the need for secrecy. 'I don't see how we can keep him here,' she said at last. 'Your Papa is bound to find out, and besides, I think he needs a doctor.'

'Davey!' The exclamation was desperate, heart-rending. 'He must stay here! Do you think they would bring him a doctor in the lock-up? Naturally they would not! Can't you bind it up somehow? You did when I broke my arm falling out of the apple tree! Oh Davey, please!'

The plea was almost too much for Miss Davidson. 'Miss Cressy, you had a doctor to set the arm! I can't do that! Binding it up is not the same!'

'Oh please try! There's no bone sticking out, is there, as there was with me.'

Miss Davidson hesitated. As far as she could tell it was a clean break, but her knowledge was limited, and she had no desire to have the young man's death on her conscience. On the other hand, Miss Cressida's argument was unanswerable. At last she turned to her and said: 'My dear, where will you sleep?'

'In there,' she answered at once, pointing to the sitting room: 'I must sleep in my apartment, Davey, so the sofa would seem to be the best place.'

Miss Davidson looked at her. She could not like the plan, and was guiltily aware that she should already be telling Sir Joshua about his daughter's scatter-brained plan, but she loved her mistress, and was, moreover, of the opinion that no good would be achieved by handing the poor young man over. She sighed.

'It doesn't seem right, Miss Cressy, to have you sleeping in there, especially with this gentleman just next door. If only there were some other way!'

'Well there isn't,' Cressida said firmly. 'And as for that talk of impropriety it's nonsense, Davey, as well you know! What harm can there possibly be? Oh, I admit Papa would have an apoplexy if he knew, but he isn't going to know, is he, Davey dear!'

Doubtfully Miss Davidson regarded her mistress. 'What happens Miss Cressy, when he wakes up? What will you tell him?'

'Nothing, of course, and neither will you! If he is a gentleman, Davey, he won't like to think he's turning a lady from her bed, and if he's not well, nothing will be served by letting him know what case he's in.' She giggled at the thought. 'Oh Davey, you must stand by me! I shall need you, you know, especially when we have to feed him! Please say yes!'

Miss Davidson, having attended Miss Cressida almost from her earliest hour, knew that eager look, and indeed, found it hard to refuse her. She smiled sourly, therefore, and said: 'I suppose I had better see about bandaging this poor boy, though the lord knows, I'm no expert!'

However this was, it was very neat work that she made of Kearsley's shoulder. Her fingers could detect nothing out of place, but she had fears, although secret, that the injury might become inflamed. She brought one of the Justice's night-shirts, smuggled out of his drawer, and after a brief struggle — she would not countenance her mistress's help — succeeded in getting her patient into it. As far as she could tell he was sleeping quite peacefully, but there was a furrow between his brows and his face was almost devoid of colour. There was no fever, however, and she allowed herself to hope that he might yet be well.

A brief tussle ensued thereafter when

Cressida tried to insist on staying in her room that evening. Nothing, she said, would give greater cause for suspicion than if the daughter of the house did not attend dinner when she was perfectly fit and healthy.

'But how do they know I'm healthy?' she demanded mutinously. 'I might just as well have the headache!'

'Yes, Miss Cressy, and you know how your father behaves when you are indisposed! That, more than anything else, would encourage him into your room! No, Miss Cressy, you must take dinner! I shall stay here with our young friend.'

And so it had to be. However much she might dislike it Cressida was forced to descend to dinner, and there she conducted herself with such charm and good humour that she succeeded in putting her father into a better mood than he had been in all day. He was not an even tempered man, and the disappearance of a rogue from under his very nose did not make for complacency. He had spent much of the early part of the evening trying to fathom out just how the fellow had escaped when he had guarded every door and searched the house throughout. Cressida, however, was his darling, and knew to perfection how to charm him out of the megrims.

He was a strict parent, but a fond one as well. He had long missed his wife in the management of his independent and headstrong daughter, but there was little he would not do to ensure her happiness either now or in the future. It was a matter of some concern that his daughter must share the house with common criminals, and he had spent more than an hour that evening in discovering who had been responsible for leaving the connecting door unlocked. An excellent supper and a cheerful daughter did much to reconcile him, and if the disappearance of the criminal returned occasionally to plague him he tried not to let it show. When the last course had been removed, however, and Cressida sat with her sweetmeats while her father enjoyed a glass of port, she raised her eyes to his face and asked carelessly: 'Who was that man today, Papa, that you were looking for?'

For a moment Sir Joshua was silent, then he set down his glass and regarded his daughter unsmilingly. 'Do you know, Cressida, I have no idea! It is really strange. According to Bedford he was definitely masked, and had all the appearance of a highwayman. Why, he even carried a pistol! But I cannot fathom why such a person should be here at all, unless to free the fellow in the lock-up, but that I find hard to believe.' He fingered the stem of his glass for a moment, and then said: 'Do you know, my dear, it is really very strange. The pistol he dropped is a very fine weapon! Of course, he might have stolen it, but it doesn't seem likely somehow. Still, I cannot imagine a highwayman with a silver-mounted fire-piece.'

'The pistol had silver mountings, Papa?'

He nodded slowly. 'It must have been stolen, of course. There is no other explanation. H.D.'

'H.D., Papa?'

'It was engraved. H.D. Most odd.'

Cressida thought it intriguing, and beguiled several minutes in trying to think up a suitable name for her mysterious gentleman. 'Tell me, Papa,' she said at last, laying down her napkin, 'when you catch this man, what will you do with him?'

Sir Joshua, whose thought had followed a different line, looked up bewildered, and then said: 'Oh, I don't know. It depends on what he's done, my dear. Of course, if he is a highwayman, as seems likely, he would probably hang.'

'Then I hope you don't catch him!' cried his daughter impetuously.

Sir Joshua looked surprised. 'You do, Cressida, what is the matter with you? Are you taking up his cause?' He laughed and looked at his daughter in amusement.

Cressida, who had by now recollected herself, blushed, and said: 'No, of course not! But it does seem hard sometimes that men are hanged for so little!'

'You would not think it little, Cressida, if you were one of the fellow's victims. But we will talk no more about it. It is not a subject for the dinner table.'

Cressida was inclined to agree, and as soon as she could she excused herself and slipped away to her apartment.

She found her maid greatly concerned. Miss Davidson was slow in opening the door, and when she did so it was obvious from her expression that all was not well. The reason was soon explained. The patient's countenance, once so pale, was now fiery red. Perspiration stood in beads on his forehead, and a deep furrow was carved between his straight dark brows.

'What is it?' Cressida asked, looking

at her maid anxiously.

'Fever,' answered Miss Davidson shortly. 'I half expected it, I must admit, but not so soon! He should have a doctor, Miss Cressy!'

'No, and no!' exclaimed the young lady, her father's words vivid in her memory. 'We shall save him, Davey, I know we shall! Give me the cloth.' Impatiently she took the cloth from her maid and gently wiped the patient's burning brow. 'I think we should rearrange his pillows,' she announced, laying aside the cloth. The maid not responding, Miss Kingman looked up sharply and said again: 'Help me, Davey!'

Reluctantly the woman came forward and carefully raised the Viscount while Cressida turned the pillows and carefully plumped them up.

'I shall sit up with him tonight,' she announced, drawing up a nearby chair.

'Oh no, Miss Cressy, that you will not do! What will your father say in the morning if you come down all heavy-eyed? I shall sit with him.'

Miss Kingman smiled. 'Very well, Davey, we'll compromise. I shall sit with him until midnight, and then you may come back. That way I shall not lose much sleep, and you will be a little refreshed. 'Now Davey,' she said, seeing her maid preparing to protest, 'I can be stubborn too! And he is my patient really, Davey dear!'

Miss Davidson smiled reluctantly. 'Very well, Miss Cressy. I can't say I shall be sorry to get my head down, but don't you go thinking I shan't come back because I shall, and on time!'

It was a very difficult two hours for Cressida. Harry was very restless, lying still for barely a minute at a time, and frequently muttering and calling out indistinguishable names and phrases. Cressida tried to determine these, hoping for some clue to his identity, but although 'Ros' was repeated frequently, she could make nothing at all of his other utterances. Once he opened his eyes and stared wildly about him, but he seemed unable to see, and soon closed them again. By the time Miss Davidson returned Cressida was very anxious, and it took a lot of coaxing to persuade her into the next room and onto the sofa.

'A fine how-de-do it would be, Miss Cressy, for you to get no sleep!' said the maid, carefully retrieving her mistress's gown from the floor. 'And what the master would say if he had any conception of this I shudder to think!' She turned to regard her mistress, demure in her long white night-dress, and smiled. 'But there, you're a girl, I know it. I'll come and tuck you up, dearie, just to see you safe.'

Cressida did not protest, but she was certain as she snuggled beneath the soft blankets that she would get no sleep that night. However that was it seemed very little time at all before she felt herself being shaken and lazily opened her eyes onto brilliant daylight.

'There now, Miss Cressy,' said the

maid, smiling. 'It's just before nine, so I must fetch your chocolate, or Cook will be wondering where I've got to!'

Cressida, wide awake now, sat up quickly and regarded her maid earnestly. 'How is he, Davey, tell me at once!'

Miss Davidson smiled. 'Asleep, my love, and resting like a babe. The fever is gone. He'll be well yet!' Had she calculated the effect of these simple words she cannot have expected her mistress to leap up and throw her arms delightedly about her neck.

'Davey, I'm so happy! You're wonderful, do you know? When you've fetched my chocolate you must get some rest, I insist.'

'Well, now, Miss, we'll talk about that later!' She smiled on the words and disappeared to fetch the chocolate. When she returned it was barely five minutes later but her mistress was already up and dressed and was carefully folding away her bedclothes.

'I couldn't wait, Davey, you see! How well he looks! I'm so proud of you!' She took the mug in both hands and carried it into the bedroom where Kearsley was sleeping quietly. 'I suppose I must get some breakfast, but after that I insist you get some rest. I can't have you all hag-eyed either!'

After a moment's hesitation Miss Davidson nodded, and Cressida, overcome for a moment, gave her a quick hug, and ran away to get her breakfast.

11

Rosamund was not asleep. In the small hours of that morning she had lain quiet but wide awake, listening for the smallest sound from the room next door that would signify her brother's return. It did not come, and shortly before seven o'clock she abandoned the attempt to sleep and got up quietly and dressed herself. She felt curiously calm. It was strange. She had been certain that when this happened she would have panicked, but no such emotion entered her breast. Her mind was strangely empty as she carefully folded her night-dress and placed it on her pillow. She walked slowly to the door, and then with little hesitation along the passage to Sir Hugh's apartment.

This gentleman was not asleep either, and he felt a stir of uneasiness as Rosamund knocked and peeped round the door. He smiled at her. 'I hope you aren't intending to make a habit of this,' he said lightly as she came across to him. 'My reputation will be in shreds!'

She smiled perfunctorily and perched herself on the end of Hugh's bed. She was finding it strangely difficult to order her thoughts, but Sir Hugh did not need to be told.

'So,' he said, repressing a sigh, 'that scoundrel has done it again!'

She smiled weakly, and nodded.

'I tell you something, Rosamund, if we three come out of this business with whole skins I shall be very much surprised!'

'What am I to do?' she asked, moving closer to him on the bed. 'I never thought I would be in a position when I was so completely at a stand, but it seems so now! Harry is missing, and I haven't the slightest idea about how to find him!'

Her voice was oddly shaky and Hugh, looking sharply into her face, was disturbed to see the glisten of unshed tears. He dragged himself up, therefore, and took hold of the hand that lay conveniently near on the counterpane. 'This is not like you,' he said, holding it in a firm grasp. 'Don't you know your brother yet? I think there is no situation that would be impossible for him, indeed I do!'

She looked at him hopefully. 'Do you? I admit, I always used to think the same way, but recently, oh, everything seems upside down!'

'Now, look here, Rose, you mustn't concern yourself. It isn't so far to Upavon, after all. What is to stop us riding out there to see for ourselves?'

She brightened a little. 'Do you think so? How ridiculous I am to get so concerned over a trifle! But are you well enough?'

He considered for a moment as she looked at him anxiously, and smiled. 'I should be very weak, you know, to be laid out any longer by a small bout of concussion! Yes, I am fit. Do you wish to go this morning?'

She nodded. 'If we might. I shan't rest, I'm afraid, until I know where he is.'

'Good! Well, I think I had better get up.' He became aware suddenly that he was still holding her hand in far too familiar a clasp and chuckled. 'If the Duchess were to see us, Rose, she would have us to the altar with very little delay!'

Rosamund laughed and slipped off the bed. 'Shall I wear breeches, Sir Hugh, or am I to be a lady today?'

Sir Hugh grimaced. 'A lady, I think. Yes, in fact I am sure.'

She nodded, content for once to let someone else make the decision. Her conversation with the baronet had comforted her strangely. As she strolled out into the corridor it occurred to her that for the first time in her life she was relying on someone else, something she had not even done in her dealings with Harry. But then, Sir Hugh was not like any other gentleman of her acquaintance. To rely on him seemed only natural. Lud, but she was a perverse creature! Who would have thought, only a few weeks ago — She shrugged her shoulders and dismissed the thought.

Rosamund spoke hardly at all throughout the drive. There was, in fact, little of relevance she could say, and in spite of Hugh's confidence she could not feel happy about Harry's chances. She sat with the rug across her knees brooding on what could possibly have happened, worrying herself almost frantic until Hugh, whose eye had been upon her for some miles past, said remorsefully: 'If I had known my company would throw you into such despondency I should never have come!'

Her head jerked up at that and she smiled, making an attempt to throw off her gravity. It soon returned, however, and almost without knowing it she fell back into reflection, a worried crease puckering her brow.

They reached Upavon at about

midday. It was not until the difficult turn through the archway had been negotiated and they had entered the courtyard that it occurred to Rosamund to ask how they were to gain access.

Sir Hugh smiled. 'Nothing clandestine, Lady Rosamund, I promise. I am reliably informed that this house is of great architectural interest, containing some of the finest Tudor panelling in the county.'

At this Rosamund gave a reluctant laugh. 'How clever you are! I declare Harry would never have thought of so simple a ruse!'

'I daresay, but it is not over yet. Your task, my dear, is to evince a violent desire to see the cells, where, you have heard, a notorious highwayman is at this moment confined.'

'You mean Harry?'

'I mean Dick, my dear, scatter-brained friend! Now keep your wits and remember to look happy!' Carefully he handed her down from the carriage and placed her wrap solicitously about her shoulders. 'I think,' he said, as he conducted her across the courtyard, 'that you should be my ward.'

She glanced up at him quickly, and then nodded. 'Am I singularly undutiful, sir? Or am I of the meek obedient sort?'

'I cannot but believe,' he retorted, 'that such a part would be beyond you! No, you shall be the impetuous, wilful type. That should suit you, I believe!' He glanced at her out of the corner of his eyes and saw her smiling. Satisfied, he drew her arm within his own and walked forward to meet the housekeeper. 'Good day,' he said, unsmilingly. 'My ward and I are putting up locally and have been reliably informed, I am sure, of the architectural excellence of this building. Is the magistrate at home?'

The housekeeper, disentangling with difficulty the meaning of Sir Hugh's words, bobbed a curtsey and said she regretted but that the master was away from home today.

Rosamund, who had been smiling eagerly, now adopted an expression of ludicrous dismay. 'From home?' she echoed. 'Oh, and I so *particularly* wanted to see the panelling! Aunt Agatha said it was so fine, too! Don't you think,' she turned to the housekeeper with a plea in her eyes, 'that we might just have a small look? We've come so far!'

'Now, Jessica,' said Hugh grimly, 'you must not bother the good lady. You heard perfectly well what she said. Good day, I am sorry to have disturbed you.'

He doffed his hat and made as if to turn round, but Rosamund caught his arm and said: 'Oh Hugh, don't be so fusty! You know how badly I want to see it, and we must get back to London tomorrow! Oh please,' here she dragged her arm away and turned back to the housekeeper, 'couldn't *you* show us over? I'm sure you would do just as well, knowing the house as intimately as you must.'

The good woman, by no means impervious to those enormous pleading brown eyes, hesitated, and then said: 'If you would step into the parlour, Miss, I shall ask the mistress if I may take you instead.'

'There, Hugh, you see!' Rosamund turned a radiant countenance on her 'guardian'. 'You are always so easily put off! Give her your card, Hugh.'

For a moment the 'guardian' looked implacable, and then he gave a quick nod, and produced with a flourish a gilt-edged card. The housekeeper received it deferentially, glanced at it, and bobbed again.

A few minutes later Miss Kingman, who was vainly trying to concentrate on a novel, was startled by a sharp rap at her door, and, glancing quickly into the bedroom, hurried across to unlock the door.

'Oh! Mrs. Hey! What is it?'

The housekeeper bobbed, and held out the card. 'A gentleman, miss, with a young lady, anxious to see over the house. I told them the master was away, but the young lady seemed so eager to see the house, Miss, I ventured to say I would ask if I might show them over.'

Cressida hesitated. 'Oh, I don't know. Are they respectable, do you think?'

'Oh yes, Miss. It's a very smart gentleman, not *young*, precisely, and a lovely young lady, his ward, I believe.'

'Well, I suppose it can't hurt, Mrs. Hey. But don't bring them along here. I don't really want to be disturbed.'

'Very good, Miss. I'm sure they will be very grateful.'

Cressida nodded, and shut the door slowly. She had the strangest feeling that all was not well, but since she could not account for this she shrugged her shoulders and returned to her seat.

Downstairs in the parlour the conspirators were nervously awaiting the outcome of Mrs. Hey's mission. A quick scrutiny of the chamber informed them that there was nothing of the slightest interest there, although Rosamund took care to be enthusing about a section of the carving as Mrs. Hey appeared again in the doorway.

There followed a boring hour. Mrs. Hey, it transpired, had been more than thirty years with the family, and her knowledge of the house and its history proved limitless. They were shown a selection of rooms ranging from drawing rooms to music rooms and bedrooms, including several galleries, sitting rooms and dining rooms. One of these rooms, a charming sitting room decorated in shades of blue and green expressly, the housekeeper informed them, for when the young mistress should wish to leave her apartments, had a large window overlooking the courtyard. Tiring of the constant flow of instructive talk Rosamund wandered to the window and stood looking down on the activity below. Behind her the instruction continued, but in a moment Sir Hugh and the housekeeper joined her.

'How interesting this is!' she said, turning with a smile to the good woman. 'There seems to be so much going on!'

'Oh yes, Miss, there's a good deal of business to do with matters of law, if you understand me. Always people in the yard here.'

Sir Hugh, mildly interested, moved to the window and peered down into the courtyard below them. As he watched a man emerged from somewhere below them and crossed the courtyard diagonally. He was a very large fellow, dressed roughly in buckskin breeches and a jerkin, with, Sir Hugh noticed, a heavy bunch of keys dangling from his waist-band.

'Who is that strong-looking fellow?' he asked curiously of the housekeeper.

'That sir, that's Faul, sir, one of the gaolers.'

Rosamund, her attention suddenly arrested, stared fixedly into the courtyard, but Sir Hugh laid a hand on her arm and drew her gently away.

Rosamund had almost begun to despair of ever finding anything useful when they came to a large, heavy oak door, studded and braced with iron, and possessing a lock and several bolts. She opened her eyes wide in awe. 'What is behind there?' she breathed, eagerly.

'The lock-ups, Miss, and not very pleasant either. Now if you would care to come this way — '

'The lock-ups!' exclaimed Rosamund, shuddering artistically. 'Do you . . . do you have any prisoners at the moment?'

Mrs. Hey had been proceeding down another passage but she turned now and answered in a tone of surprise: 'Why yes, Miss, and a rascally fellow he is, too! The master was very lucky to catch him.'

Sir Hugh, casting Rosamund a warning glance, said: 'I'm glad to hear it. There are far too many villains at large. I only wish more might be caught!'

'Yes, sir, so do we all!'

'You only have the one, then, at the moment?' Rosamund asked, a little anxiously.

'Yes, Miss, just the one.'

'May I see him? I've never seen a highwayman!' She gave a little laugh, but the nervous quality of her voice caused the housekeeper to look at her curiously.

'Jessica, you do not want to see the highwayman,' said Sir Hugh, looking meaningfully at her. 'He is doubtless a rogue.'

'Oh yes, sir, that he is! Chuffy Dick they call him, though why I can't conceive, for a more unpleasant-looking fellow you never met with!'

'I should still like to see him,' persisted Rosamund obstinately.

'Come, Jessica, I do not wish it!'

She glanced up at him in surprise, for the message in his voice was unmistakable.

'Come!'

Puzzled, but willing, she took his arm and allowed him to lead her away.

There followed only the library and the magistrate's study, at which they were allowed a brief look, as at the scene of Chuffy Dick's appearance a few days earlier.

'Not that there was any doubt of his guilt,' said Mrs. Hey, closing the door firmly on that interesting room. 'They caught him in the act, as it were, so there was no chance of his wriggling out of it.'

Rosamund opened her mouth to speak, but at that instant there came the sound of rending material and she found her progress suddenly impeded. The reason was obvious. As she glanced back she saw Sir Hugh hurriedly remove his foot from a large section of muslin flounce, and heard him say: 'Indeed, Jessica, you should take more care of your clothes!'

She was about to protest, and then, thinking it might not be accidental after all, gave an exclamation of dismay and bent down to examine the damage. This appeared to be considerable. Hugh had done his job well and a section of skirt hung free about half way round the bottom of her gown. 'It must have been a nail,' she said ruefully. 'Do you think — do you think I could have something to pin it up? I don't think I can get home like this!'

'Oh dear, that *is* a bad tear, and such a pretty gown! Would you care to wait in the parlour and I shall see what I can find.'

'Jessica, why do you not go with the good lady? I shall wait for you in the parlour.'

The housekeeper smiled. 'Perhaps it would be as well! I'm not sure a pin would be of much use, sir, as torn as it is! I'll ask Mr. Walker to bring you some wine, sir.'

'Do not trouble. I shall be well enough.'

She curtseyed, and Rosamund, with one backward, mischievous glance, followed in her wake.

Sir Hugh had opened the door to the parlour as if to enter but no sooner had they disappeared from view than he shut the door again carefully and walked quickly and quietly back along the passage. He hesitated a moment between two doors and then selected one, and slipped into the magistrate's study.

It was a large room, dark, with much heavy panelling around the walls. It was obtrusively tidy, the desk being almost bare but for a standish and a small pile of unused paper. Rapidly Sir Hugh scanned the room, dismissing at once the various cabinets and shelves, and crossed purposefully to the broad leather-topped desk. It contained several shallow drawers, but an examination of each revealed little of interest. More papers, and several quills were to be found, but no ring. The lower drawer, however, provided him with something more significant. It was locked. Hurriedly he sorted through the drawers again, but no key was apparent. There seemed no help for it. He caught up a long steel paper knife, and inserted it carefully in the gap between drawer and rim. Sliding it back and forth it met the obstruction of the lock, and with more haste than care he jerked it suddenly against the metal, causing the lock to spring back with a snap. Cautiously he opened the drawer. It proved to contain an interesting miscellany of items, mostly valueless and unimportant. A quick search assured him that the ring was not there, and he was about to close the drawer when the largest object which he had several times moved from one side to the other at last attracted his notice. It was a pistol, and one which he had last seen when it was levelled threateningly at his forehead. Any slight doubt he might have felt as to its ownership was quickly dispelled by a cursory examination, which revealed the initials H.D. Thoughtfully he ran a finger over the engraved monogram, and then recollecting his situation he put it carefully back into its former position and shut the drawer. There was no way in which he could lock the drawer, and he must hope the magistrate would assume he had merely been careless, and would not notice the slight scratches on the polished mahogany. Greatly troubled he crossed the room and listened for a moment before gently opening the door. He had barely gained the parlour before he heard Rosamund's voice raised unusually as she and the housekeeper came back along the passage.

'I'm *so* grateful,' she was saying loudly. 'I can't imagine *how* I came to do such a thing! My best muslin, too! However, I'm sure it will be well. My maid has a marvellous way with mending, you know. I declare I can never see her stitches except in the strongest light!'

They had by this time gained the door and Rosamund, fervently hoping that her 'guardian' was once more within, allowed the housekeeper to usher her in.

'Ah, Hugh,' she exclaimed to the

figure by the window. 'So fortunate! Mrs. Hey was good enough to tack it up for me so it will be fine until I can get Jenny to mend it for me. I hope you haven't been too bored!'

He turned and regarded her coldly. 'No, but I will thank you to take more care of your possessions in future. Shall we go?' He extended his arm with an air of authority and turned to the housekeeper. 'Pray convey my compliments and thanks to your mistress. A most charming house.'

The housekeeper bobbed, and held open the door for them to pass through.

'I hope you never mean to subject me to such again,' whispered Rosamund fiercely as they crossed the courtyard towards the carriage. 'I was never more bored in my life!'

Sir Hugh smiled, but said: 'For my part I am exceedingly glad you are not my ward! A more troublesome piece I could not hope to find!'

'Thank you! I can imagine what

miserable life I should lead under your roof!'

With this exchange of pleasantries they gained their carriage and Hugh, preserving his severity of countenance with a little difficulty, handed her in gravely and climbed in himself.

Barely had the door been shut upon them before Rosamund turned to her companion and said eagerly: 'Well, what did you find?'

'No ring, I'm afraid, and I'm certain, too, that he is not in the lock-up.'

'I agree, but where is he, then?'

Sir Hugh frowned. 'I don't know. But he was there, that much is sure.'

'He was? How do you know? Oh, do tell me, please!'

Sir Hugh looked at her. 'I found his pistol,' he replied, 'in the desk in the study, a silver-mounted piece inscribed H.D.'

'Henry Daviot! Yes, that is his! So he was there, and met with some trouble, too! But where is he now?'

Sir Hugh shook his head, and at that

moment the carriage lurched forward over the cobbles. 'I have not the slightest idea,' he replied frankly. 'He was there, he met some trouble, and presumably escaped, since he is not there now!'

'Oh, I wish you had let me see the lock-up!' Rosamund said agitatedly. 'I'm sure we would have learnt something!'

'And I am sure we would not! No, Rose, it would not have done. Did you want to attract attention to us by such an outlandish thing?'

'No, but — Sir Hugh, what are you doing?'

The baronet had leant forward suddenly and banged on the roof. 'I'm sure that's the gaoler we just passed,' he said, opening the door as the carriage drew up. 'If it is we might yet learn something.'

Peering out Rosamund saw that they had passed a man on foot walking along the grass verge with a large bundle in one hand. She recognised him easily as the fellow she had seen in the courtyard.

'Halloa!' called Sir Hugh as the fellow approached them. 'Can we take you up?'

The man had touched his forelock at Sir Hugh's greeting and now seemed genuinely surprised. 'Why, thankee, sir, but I'm only goin' to Everleigh, to visit my brother. 'Tis not above five miles, sir.'

'Get in, my good man, 'tis no trouble.'

Bewildered the man watched as Sir Hugh jumped into the road and held open the door, indicating him to climb in. Approaching the carriage he touched his forelock again and said: 'Indeed, sir, I'm much obliged, but — '

He got no further. Sir Hugh, no weakling, gave him a sharp push in the small of his back, and by dexterously kicking his legs away from beneath him succeeded in sending him face down onto the floor of the carriage. Rosamund totally unprepared, gave a startled cry, to which Hugh paid not the slightest heed, merely climbing in after the fellow and adjuring the astonished coachman somewhat agitatedly to 'put 'em along'.

Considerably startled, and not a little disturbed, the gaoler picked himself up and rather unsteadily gained the backward seat. Being engaged in brushing the dust from his breeches he did not immediately look up, but when he did he found himself staring into the muzzle of a plain, but serviceable pistol, drawn, to Rosamund's surprise, from the holster a few minutes earlier.

'Please, sir, don't shoot, I beg of you! What d'you want wi' me? I haven't any money!'

'My good fellow,' said Sir Hugh, reclining at his leisure against the squabs, 'I have not the slightest desire to rob you. Search him, please. He might have something concealed.'

Mystified but obedient, Rosamund exchanged her seat for the one opposite and with practised hands delved into the various pockets that adorned the man's apparel. 'Just this,' she said, drawing forth a stout cudgel.

'Good,' said Sir Hugh, receiving it from her and throwing it carelessly from the carriage. 'And now, my friend, a little information, if you please!'

'Sir, I don't know anything! What can I know?'

'The whereabouts of a certain person who invaded the privacy of the magistrate's house sometime yesterday afternoon.'

Fervently the fellow shook his head. 'You're makin' a mistake! I don't know anything!'

'My friend, you lie.' Turning to Rosamund he said curtly: 'Hold this pistol. If he stirs an inch kill him.'

Rosamund, somewhat to the gaoler's surprise, received the weapon readily, and held it with an ease that suggested she had every knowledge of how to use it. Satisfied that Rosamund was well in command Sir Hugh joined the gaoler on the opposite seat.

'I really think you might tell us,' he said softly, eyeing the fellow with a decided gleam in his eye. 'I should not like to have to . . . er . . . persuade you!'

While the threat was not lost on the fellow, he had yet some doubts of its being put into execution, so he shook his head stubbornly and folded his arms. Suddenly, and considerably to Rosamund's surprise — she had always judged him to be a mild-tempered man — Sir Hugh had landed what, in the right circles, would be known as a facer, sending the unfortunate victim crashing against the side of the carriage and making Rosamund glad she was no longer occupying that seat. At once Sir Hugh was bending over the fellow in a threatening manner, demanding to be told what he wanted to know. The gaoler, meanwhile, had been thinking hard, and he had decided that if this villain was prepared to go to such lengths to discover such a thing then there must be a reason for keeping it concealed, and he determined not to let these rascals discover what had happened for as long as he could help it. This was perhaps an unfortunate decision. Sir Hugh, driven on by grim determination and the knowledge that if he did not elicit the information Rosamund certainly would, applied himself with vigour to the task of discovery, alternately threatening and cajoling, and generally getting nowhere. At last he sat down again beside Rosamund and subjected the gaoler to his scrutiny.

'Well, my dear, what do you think?'

'I wish you would leave it to me,' she suggested wistfully. 'I'm sure I could discover something.'

Strangely enough the idea of being interrogated by this unnatural girl disturbed the gaoler much more than all Sir Hugh's threats had done. He eyed her apprehensively and said nothing.

'Do you know,' said Rosamund, who had been contemplating the fellow thoughtfully, 'I believe I have hit upon an idea! How about if we took all his clothes and put him back on the highway. That should be punishment enough, I think.'

Sir Hugh chuckled and cocked an eyebrow at the gaoler. 'An ugly-looking customer, though, don't you think? But perhaps not a bad idea.'

Rosamund nodded and handed the pistol back to Sir Hugh. Moving across she favoured the unfortunate victim with a charming smile that seemed perfectly horrific to that individual, and lifted her hands to the spotted kerchief he wore. With a swift movement she had ripped it away, causing the fellow to blush fiery and jerk one hand to his throat. The action caused Sir Hugh to raise the pistol dangerously and say harshly: 'Sit still, if you value your skin.'

The fellow shrank back and began to jabber, but Rosamund's eyes were fixed on something hanging about the fellow's neck.

'Sir,' she said, in a strange, high-pitched voice, 'would you come over here?'

Self-consciously the gaoler raised his hand to his throat, but Hugh, after giving Rosamund one puzzled glance, calmly and firmly removed the hand and looked at what had so nearly rendered his accomplice speechless.

A string hung about the fellow's neck, rough and untidily knotted. What depended from it was hidden now by the shirt, but even as Sir Hugh drew it forth he knew what he would find. It was a ring. A large emerald, it hung heavily on its string, glittering and winking with a fire all its own. Sir Hugh drew his breath in sharply and regarded the fellow coldly.

'Well, my friend, this is an unfortunate day for you! Where had you this ring?'

'It's mine!' he protested in a tight, high voice. 'I had it from my father.'

'Did you indeed! Perhaps you would explain why it adorns your neck and not your finger?'

'My w-work,' stammered the fellow unhappily. 'I'd lose it if they saw it.'

'Ay, as did Dick, did he not? So, you took it from him, in return for what, I wonder? What did you promise him?'

The gaoler looked from one to the other and sighed miserably. 'I don't know what you want!' he protested feebly. 'Why can't you leave me alone?'

Sir Hugh laughed. 'My dear fellow, you have only to tell me what you know and you will be free!'

'M-my ring!' said the fellow, making a futile grab for it as Sir Hugh held it away.

'I would not, if I were you,' Hugh said coldly. 'This ring could easily put you in prison, my friend, if I were to tell what I know.'

'W-what you know?' faltered the gaoler, his wide eyes darting from one face to the other.

'You see, my friend,' drawled Sir Hugh, absently fingering the emerald, 'I know from whom Dick had this! It's an heirloom, my friend. I fear you made a bad choice. Put it away,' he said to Rosamund, 'and for the lord's sake keep it safe!'

She smiled, but said: 'What of this fellow?'

'Well, you know, he still has not told us what he knows,' said Hugh, smiling a little at the gaoler's discomfort. 'I think, however, if he were to tell us we might consider letting him go.'

'And what about the ring?' squeaked the gaoler, breathing a little faster.

'That is forfeit, my friend. The penalty for your folly. Now, the person who broke into Sir Joshua's house.'

The gaoler nodded weakly. 'There was someone, a man, masked he was, and nasty with it. Tried to shoot me! Would have killed me, too, if 'is pistol hadn't been empty.'

'What happened to him?' Rosamund demanded.

'I don't know, sure to God I don't! Vanished, he did, although we searched the house right through! He ain't there, I swear it!'

'For your sake,' said Sir Hugh, 'I hope you are right! Now, if you breathe a word of this, my friend, I shall not hesitate to lay an information that you stole this ring from its rightful owner. It would not go well for you, I fear.'

The gaoler swallowed, and looked hesitantly from one to the other. 'Can — can I go now?'

Sir Hugh considered. 'It seems a shame to part with so promising a specimen, but yes, I suppose we must let you go!' With that he banged on the roof with the pistol and moved back to his own side. A few seconds later the gaoler with his pack and neck-tie, found himself deposited, none too carefully, upon the King's highway, and the coach, with its two barbarous occupants rumbled off again into the distance.

Inside the coach all was silence. Sir Hugh, having returned the unloaded pistol to its holster, sat thoughtfully polishing his quizzing glass while Rosamund in the other corner stared out of the window, her fingers absently twisting the emerald back and forth.

'Not altogether a wasted day,' said Sir Hugh at last, ceasing his polishing and turning to look at his companion.

Rosamund glanced down at the emerald, and then across at Sir Hugh. 'How strange life is! Only yesterday I should have been so relieved to have this — this *wretched* thing in my possession, and now — ' she gave a short laugh — 'I don't seem to care whether I have it or not!'

'He is not at the house,' said Sir Hugh.

'No.'

'We'll find him, Rose. We must do, you know. After all, where can he have gone?'

She looked up now, her eyes bright and troubled. 'That's just it! There isn't anywhere, unless he went home, and why should he do that? No, I'm sure there's something wrong! There must be, Hugh, don't you see?'

He did see, but he said reassuringly: 'We have no way of telling what might have happened. He got away, that we do know.'

'Yes,' said Rosamund bitterly, 'but he might be hurt, or even dead! At least if he had been taken I should know what I was up against, but this is dreadful!'

'Rose, do you seriously think he is dead?'

She looked at him for a moment, and then shook her head. 'No. I think I would know. But I can't get it out of my head that he has been hurt, and it makes me so uneasy! We've been so close, you know. In fact, I can't remember when we have been apart for as much as a day!'

'Then if he is alive we shall find him,' said Hugh firmly. 'What has happened to your resolution?'

She gave a shaky laugh. 'Heaven knows! I hope it returns before too long or I shall be useless!'

'You will never be that, as well you

know. What are you holding in your hand?'

She glanced down at the ring, and smiled. 'I'm so glad that poor man told us what we needed to know! I should never have got much further!'

Sir Hugh laughed and took her hand. 'I believe you would, you know! So much for your lack of resolution!'

She smiled gratefully up at him. 'How kind you are! We really do not deserve such goodness, Harry and I. What we would have done without you I dare not think.'

'You would have managed, as you always have done, I don't doubt, just as you will manage now.'

'Well, I hope you may be right.'

'I hope so too,' said Sir Hugh bracingly. 'I'm not as experienced in these matters as you seem to think! In fact, without you I doubt if I should get far at all.'

12

What a warm and comfortable bed it was, Harry thought, snuggling down a little deeper. How strange that he had never noticed it before! It almost made him want to stay there all day. Still, nothing was achieved by slug-a-beds, and he lazily raised one eye-lid.

He was lying on his back but with his head turned sideways on the pillow, and consequently he had a full and perfect view of a truly lovely countenance, heart-shaped, and surrounded by a myriad of golden curls. She was not looking at him, but seemed to be concentrating on something on her lap, for her lips were parted slightly and the movement of her eyelids showed that she was reading. As he watched her, fascinated, she drew in her breath sharply, and, raising one hand to her mouth, continued to read avidly. It must have been an exceedingly good book, thought Harry idly, wondering vaguely what she was doing at his bedside. Not that he was averse to her presence, oh no, for it must always be a pleasure to waken from deep slumber and find an angel at one's bedside. He continued to look at her, his mind ceasing to ponder the mystery of her presence, and as he looked he thought suddenly that she was vaguely familiar. He frowned over it, but the effort of concentration proved too much and he soon gave it up. Instead he snuggled down a little further, and as he did so the most excruciating pain he had ever known was set up in his shoulder, causing him to let out a cry of real anguish. The girl was up in an instant and bending over him with such a look of concern in her great violet-blue eyes that Harry felt impelled to laugh, wincing at the same time with the agony in his shoulder.

'You must lie still!' exclaimed the girl, laying one hand kindly but firmly on his good shoulder. 'You have a bad injury, you know, and if you wriggle it will never mend!'

He raised one brow at her. 'Broken bone, eh? Well, I must admit it feels devilish.'

'Of course it does! What else would you expect? But it's healing nicely now, and the inflammation seems to have gone right down. At least, that's what Davey says.'

'And who might Davey be?' inquired Harry, focusing his eyes with a little difficulty on her face.

'She's . . . she's your nurse, sir, and she will be so angry when she sees how you have disturbed your pillows. Let me arrange them for you.'

Obediently Harry submitted to being lifted gently and having his pillows plumped and straightened, biting his lip as a dagger shot down his arm. He smiled as she set him down, however, and felt emboldened to ask where he was.

Cressida hesitated. 'You . . . you're

at my father's house,' she said.

He smiled at her. 'And who might your father be?' he inquired genially.

'All these questions! You must stay quiet, you know, if you are to get better!'

'Very well, if you don't wish to tell me where I am perhaps you would tell me how I happened to break my shoulder.'

Again she hesitated, her lips parted anxiously.

As she did not answer he frowned, and said sharply: 'Who are you?'

She blushed now and her eyes fell beneath the fire of his gaze. 'I . . . I . . . '

'You're going to have to tell me, you know,' he said pleasantly, 'or were you planning to keep me permanently in the dark?'

'Oh no!' she exclaimed, shaking her head agitatedly. 'It's not that at all! It's just . . . well, Davey said you mustn't get excited, you see, and I'm afraid you will be very angry when you know!'

'I think you must tell me now,' Harry said, eyeing her coolly.

'Yes. Well, I suppose I must. You are in my father's house, as I told you.'

'And your father is?'

'Sir Joshua Kingman.'

Harry's eyes widened for a moment and then he relaxed back onto his pillows. 'I see. Sir Joshua Kingman. I feel I should know — Good God!' he exclaimed, struggling now to get on to his good elbow. 'I must get away! Madam, I am sure you intend well, but you do not realise what you are doing!'

'Oh I do, indeed I do,' cried Cressida, tears starting to her eyes. 'Oh please lie down, sir! You will do yourself such damage!'

Surprised by the earnestness of her appeal Harry regarded her gravely, but relaxed again after a moment. 'Perhaps you will tell me, then, what I am doing here.'

'You . . . you hurt your shoulder, your collar-bone, Davey says, and we are looking after you. You are really quite safe.'

'In a Justice's house?' He laughed shortly. 'Indeed, ma'am, can my disreputable calling truly have escaped your notice?'

Her eyes fell and she studied her finger-tips. 'No. I know you are — a highwayman, sir, but that does not weigh with me!' She raised her enormous eyes to his face and said earnestly: 'I wish you would tell me who you are!'

He laughed now with genuine amusement and reaching out caught hold of her hand. 'So you truly do not care! I am Harry, sweet fair. And by what name must I address an angel?'

She blushed rosily and drew back the hand. 'I am Miss Kingman, sir.'

'Miss Kingman, indeed! Now, now, sweet life, you can do better than that! Am I to call you Miss Kingman all my days?'

She met his bantering look and smiled shyly. 'Cressida.'

'Cressida.' He weighed it on his tongue and seemed pleased. 'Well, Miss Cressida Kingman, and are you going to tell me my fate?'

'Your fate, sir?' she faltered, opening her eyes wide.

He repressed a sigh. 'I lie abed in a Justice's house, my calling is known, and yet you seem not to understand me! When shall I hang?'

The eyes flashed at that. 'Never, sir, while I can help it!'

'Oh, well said, sweet life, but not enough, I fear, to save me from the noose! Or have you a mind to take up my cause?'

She considered him for a moment, and then perched on the edge of his bed. 'Do you remember nothing?'

For an instant it seemed as though he would repudiate the question, but then he frowned and said: 'I remember coming here; I remember, too, why I came. But — Wait, I have it! That fellow hit me! My pistol was unloaded and the fellow struck me.

I remember staggering — Lord, but it was painful! — and a door, falling through a door — ' He stopped and looked up at the anxious face above him. 'I came to your room,' he said slowly. 'Can it truly be — No!' He laughed at the thought.

'What?' she demanded eagerly. 'What are you thinking?'

'Sweet life, have you truly concealed me in your chamber?'

The colour flooded her cheeks and she looked down at her hands, clasping and unclasping in her lap.

'Good God!' he exclaimed, thunderstruck. 'You have! And your father does not know?'

She shook her head.

For a moment he looked at her, amazed, and then he chuckled, softly at first, and then louder. 'Lord, here's a pretty coil! Upon my word, it's famous! Concealed from a Justice in his own house!' The laugh died, and he regarded her with concern. 'But my dear, the risks you have run! How long have I been here?'

'Two nights,' she answered in a small voice, not daring to look at him.

'Two nights!' he repeated hollowly. 'My God, Cressida, you must help me to get up, to dress!'

She was on her feet now, gently pressing him back onto the pillows. 'Oh please, please lie still, I beg of you! You have no idea what you are saying! You cannot leave until you are quite fit!'

'Cressida, how can you keep me here any longer? Besides, I have friends, and they will be so worried about me I shudder to think what they might not do!'

'I wish you would let me help you,' she said in a small voice, looking at him pleadingly.

Harry looked up at the enormous violet eyes, so kind and yet so anxious, and felt a most peculiar sensation somewhere in the region of his stomach. 'Very well,' he said at last. 'I am more indebted to you than you can possibly conceive! Tell me what you would have me do.'

'Only lie quiet for a few minutes! It is all I ask? I shall fetch you some broth, or some such thing, Davey will know, and then you will feel better. After that, if you like, you may tell me what your trouble is, and I shall see what can be done for you. Perhaps I can go to your friends?'

He nodded, quite overcome by the selflessness of the girl. 'Thank you,' he said simply, taking her hand again in a light, firm clasp. She smiled, blushed, and silently withdrew.

Left alone Harry was able to review the situation. Although he was apparently safe for the present it seemed unlikely that he would be so for long, and his safety depended on his conveying a message to Rosamund who would, he well knew, be frantic by now. His gratitude when he thought of what Cressida had done for him was enormous, and how to repay her without involving her in some sordid scandal he knew not. But it was plain to him from the agony in his shoulder that he would be going nowhere that day, or, it was probable, the following day either. If only he could somehow alleviate the pressure on Miss Kingman! This must be dreadful, he decided, and as he considered it, the fact that she had managed to keep him concealed so long drew his admiration. In fact there was only one other woman he knew who would attempt such a thing and that was his sister. This naturally drew his thoughts back to one of his more pressing concerns. Rosamund was bound to look for him, and since she knew him as she did, would be bound to come to Upavon. And what would she find? Nothing, naturally. And what then? Daviot, of course, but after that? It was a complete blank. Harry knew his sister too well to think she would panic, but she would be worried to distraction by his absence.

And then, too, there was that accursed ring!

Fortunately, just as he was about to consider this knotty problem the door opened and he jerked up his head to see a tall spare woman in early middle-age bearing a tray on which reposed a bowl of no doubt disgusting sustenance.

'Well, sir,' said this good woman in reproving accents, 'so you are awake at last! And a fine time you gave us, let me tell you, sleeping for so long! Delirious, too, for some of the time! I've brought you some chicken broth, some of Cook's best, and it's to be hoped she doesn't miss it, for I had to sneak it away while she was with Mrs. Hey. But it's good, heartening stuff, sir, and warm, too, as I daresay you'll like.' Carefully she set it down on a nearby table and moved across to the bed. 'Now, sir, I'm sure that between us we can contrive to get you into a sitting position, don't you, for feeding you flat on your back is more than I'm prepared to do!'

Harry grinned, and helpfully levered

himself onto his good elbow, enabling Miss Davidson to stack the pillows at his back. 'You're very good to me, Miss — '

'Davidson, but the child calls me Davey.'

' — Miss Davidson! What I should have done without you I dare not think!'

'No, and you shall not, while I have anything to say! Thinking never did a particle of good to any mortal, so take heed and drink your broth.'

'Yes, Davey,' said Harry meekly, his lively eyes twinkling at her.

'Ah, you're a wicked boy, I might have guessed!' she exclaimed, carefully setting the tray upon his knees. 'And stealing my dear one's heart, I'll be bound, and her an innocent!'

At that Harry frowned, and laid down the spoon. 'You'll get no bad proposals from me, Miss Davidson, and that I can promise! I know I look a rogue, but — '

'Now then!' interrupted Miss Davidson

severely. 'Talking is not allowed! Besides, we know you're a gentleman right enough, though what you want with gallivanting in black masks is more than *I* can understand! However, that's neither here nor there! The business is to get you mended and on your feet, and Miss Cressy back in her room with no harm done!'

'Are you telling me I've turned Miss Kingman from her bed?' he demanded suddenly.

'Well, sir, and where do you think it is you are? Upon my word, and I took you for a downy one!'

He grinned at her. 'It seems at the moment you're right out there! However, I wish you had not let me take her bed. I'd as lief have slept on the floor!'

'And had all the world falling over you? Fie on you, sir! The lamb's been comfortable enough, I've seen to that, though I must admit I've had the devil's own task keeping her from sitting up all night with you, so

281

concerned as she was for your health!'

Harry sipped his broth and said: 'I cannot imagine how you managed it! What of the maids? Did they not want to clean?'

'Ay, they did, but I took care of them. Silly chits, they are, giggling and gossiping! Glad of any chance to skimp their work. But you're not to worry yourself about those things, sir! There's enough on your mind, I can see right enough.'

He nodded and returned the empty bowl. 'I must get a message to my friends. Like as not they're scouring the countryside for me. I see well that I cannot get up, but can a message be taken? They are at Ashbourne.'

'Ashbourne!' Her brows flew up and she regarded her patient keenly. 'You're not the young Duke, are you?'

He laughed. 'No, Davey, I'm not a Duke, although if my luck holds and I live that long I shall be an Earl one day!'

'An Earl, indeed! Well, I knew you

were Quality-make right enough when I saw your shirt! But an Earl!' She shook her head.

An embarrassing thought occurred to Harry. 'Forgive me inquiring, but just who was responsible for putting me to bed? Not Miss Kingman, I hope!'

'Lord have mercy! What are you thinking me, sir? Of course she did not! I did it myself!'

'Well, that seems just as bad!'

'Nonsense! You're little more than a child!'

He grinned at her. 'I certainly feel little more at present.'

'Ah,' nodded Miss Davidson approvingly. 'That's how you should feel! Do what you're told and you'll not be laid up above a fortnight.'

'A fortnight!' he ejaculated, staring at her. 'Ma'am, I am exceedingly grateful for the help you've given me, but you seriously do not think you can conceal me so long!'

'No, I do not,' she answered calmly, 'but you'll be so good as not to worry

Miss Cressy with such things. It's a time I've had already persuading her you're not dying without you putting other notions into her head. There's time enough for us to worry ourselves over that.'

He nodded, and watched in silence as she picked up the tray and left the room. A few minutes later Cressida reappeared, pleased that he had eaten his broth and was apparently feeling so much better.

'But I do wish you would tell me who you are,' she said wistfully, twisting her sash back and forth between her fingers. 'Davey says you are an Earl!'

He laughed. 'No, sweet life, merely a Viscount! Kearsley. My father is the Earl of Carston.'

Cressida opened her eyes and looked at him in amazement. 'Good gracious! So you are not a highwayman after all!'

'I fear I am, my dear, and successful enough to be convicted at the next quarter sessions.'

'But the Earl of Carston!' she protested, staring at him. 'Why, even I have heard of him, and you know, I have spent most of my time in Bath recently at a stuffy seminary.'

'The fact that I am Carston's son does not mean I may not be a robber also,' Harry explained gently.

'But I don't understand,' Cressida said wretchedly, perching on the edge of the bed. 'What made you do such a silly thing? It can't have been the money!'

'No, it wasn't the money.'

'Then what?'

He sighed and met her inquiring gaze. 'The excitement,' he said at last. 'The need for . . . for adventure, for something different, I don't know! Life is so *dull*, Cressida, with nothing but estates to manage and ride around! If my father would let me go to London — but it is useless. I know he would not. He would say I was too extravagant, and I have to admit,' he said, grinning suddenly, 'that I probably would be!'

'Well, I can understand you wanting excitement,' said Cressida, 'but to risk so much! Was there nothing else you could do?'

He shrugged. 'I daresay a thousand things, but Ros and I seemed to have done most of them. We got into some rare scrapes, I can tell you!'

'Who is Ros?' Cressida asked carelessly, but with a sharp look at the Viscount.

He grinned. 'My twin, sweet life, fear not! And such a girl! I wish you could meet her, Cressy, there's nothing she would not do. I can trust her as I trust no other.'

Cressida thought this was perhaps the best thing she had heard anyone say of another, and could not repress the wish that someone might say it of her. 'I wish I could meet her too.'

'Perhaps you will,' said Harry, regarding her kindly. 'I daresay you would hit it off famously. I know perfectly well she will love you just for saving me!'

Cressida blushed and said, 'It was not so very much!'

He took her hand at this and said: 'My dear heart, were it not for you I would certainly be awaiting trial at this moment, and may yet, for all I can see.'

'Oh no, no!' she exclaimed, tightening her clasp on his hand. 'They will not take you, I promise! Have I not kept you well until now?'

Harry, his heart strangely twisted by her anxiety, gave her hand a quick squeeze and released it. 'Yes, well, I daresay all will yet be well with me.'

'It will not, you know, if you do not give up those silly starts!' she told him severely.

Harry laughed. 'Do you really care?' he asked.

'Of course I care! How can you ask such a thing when I have spent the last two days nursing you?'

He shrugged. 'I wouldn't blame you,

you know, if you washed your hands of me.'

'Well, I'm sure that is what Papa would advise me to do,' she admitted frankly, 'and to own the truth, if you intend carrying on with this silliness I feel very much inclined to let Justice take its course!'

He opened his eyes wide. 'Deliver me up, my sweet? After so much trouble?'

'Well no, perhaps not that, but I certainly would not feel inclined to do the same again!' she declared, her eyes flashing at him.

Harry grinned. 'So severe! And what will I do with myself, I wonder, when all this is over?'

She glanced at him quickly, and then away again. 'How can I tell that?' she answered carelessly. 'Other people manage, why shouldn't you?'

He sighed. 'Dearest Cressida, I fear you do not know me! I cannot spend my days in contemplation of my inheritance!'

She turned her great violet eyes upon him. 'Could you not try?'

Harry did not reply. A warning bell had just been triggered in his brain, and as he looked at her he felt it would be prudent at that moment to withdraw. 'You should not concern yourself with me,' he answered shortly, stirring restlessly beneath the covers. 'I am what I am. Nothing will change me. Now, may I write that note?'

The rebuke in his voice was obvious. She stood up and regarded him reproachfully. 'I am sorry,' she managed at last. 'I did not mean to interfere.'

'Wait!' Harry cried as she turned to go. 'Forgive me, I did not mean to be so rude! It's just that I don't want you worrying about me!' She looked at him silently, and he smiled. 'I daresay I shall not be so foolish again,' he said. 'After all, one such experience as this is enough for any man!'

'If only you meant it,' she sighed, sadly.

Harry hesitated. He felt himself to be

getting into deep waters, but it seemed too late to turn back. 'I do mean it,' he said at last. 'I shall not rob again. The lord knows what I shall do with myself, but I promise I shall not.'

Of a sudden her face was wreathed in smiles. 'Truly? You really mean it?' He nodded. 'Oh sir, you do not know how relieved I am!' She moved towards him and caught his hand impulsively. 'I do not think I could bear it if you were taken now,' she told him shyly, blushing, and turning her face away.

'Well, with luck I shall be well yet, but I must get a message to my sister.'

Cressida nodded. 'Of course. If she is the daughter of an Earl there will not be the slightest query about my sending someone to Daviot with a note.'

'Thank you, but she is not at Daviot. She and a friend, Sir Hugh Eavleigh, are at Ashbourne, with the Duchess.'

'Who did you say?'

'The Duchess of Ashbourne.'

'No, no, the friend. Who was the friend?'

'Eavleigh. Sir Hugh Eavleigh.'

Cressida regarded him frowningly for a moment, and then jumped up, saying: 'Wait a moment, I'm sure I've heard that name before!' She disappeared on the words, leaving Harry mystified for as long as a minute when she returned with a white card in her fingers. 'See!' she cried triumphantly. 'Sir Hugh Eavleigh! He was here, I'm sure of it, only yesterday.'

'Sir Hugh?' echoed Harry sharply, sitting up.

'Yes. I'm positive. Oh, I didn't see him, but I'm certain Mrs. Hey took round a gentleman of that name. He had his ward with him. Oh!' She looked at the Viscount, who nodded in confirmation.

'My sister, I would imagine. I wonder what they found?'

'Why, nothing, I would suppose, as you were up here all the time with me. I never saw them myself.'

'No. That wasn't what I meant, but no matter. May I write that note?'

'You may not,' Cressida said firmly, 'but I shall write it for you, if you will let me.'

He grinned at her. 'Thank you! I shall tell you just what to say.'

★ ★ ★

Despondently Sir Hugh allowed himself to be divested of his greatcoat and absently removed a speck of dust from his dark blue sleeve. He was quite at a loss. Two days of scouring the countryside had produced nothing more significant than a stray mare, its reins tied to a broken and dangling branch, found wandering some miles away at Collingbourne Kingston. At first Rosamund had been inclined to consider the event with foreboding, until it was pointed out that the animal had obviously been tethered, had broken free, and could have wandered many miles from where Harry had left her. All the same, the discovery seemed to argue some ill-fated venture, and Hugh had had difficulty in dissuading Rosamund from riding to Upavon at once. Having mechanically straightened his wrist bands, his brow thoughtfully wrinkled, Sir Hugh proceeded slowly to the drawing room where he knew perfectly well Rosamund would be awaiting his arrival. He was at a loss to know what to tell her. It did not seem possible that the full sum of his investigation was precisely nothing, and yet that was how it was. Harry had been at Upavon, that was certain; it seemed probable too, that it was from here that Sally had broken free. Harry had disappeared. He had been in the house, and had vanished, and although the premises had been thoroughly searched no trace of him had been discovered. Weighing the evidence slowly and carefully there seemed but one possible answer — that Harry, whether dead or alive, was still at Upavon. It was this realisation that Hugh almost dreaded telling Rosamund. What would be her reaction he could not conceive, but it seemed likely that she would be spurred by that activity that had characterised her life until now.

Even before he spoke Rosamund knew he had found nothing. The gravity in his kind grey eyes told her everything, and she nodded in tacit understanding. Without a word Sir Hugh moved across to the wine table and poured two glasses of sherry from the decanter that was standing there.

'I know he's alive,' said Rosamund, receiving the glass thankfully. 'And I think he is almost well again. When you came in just now I had been trying to decide what I really felt about this, and indeed, I can't find it in me to worry any more! Don't ask me to explain it, for I can't. It's just one of those feelings I get sometimes. I know he is all right.'

Considerably relieved Sir Hugh disposed his length in a comfortable armchair. 'He must still be there,' he said at last.

Rosamund nodded. 'I know. I've thought around it in every way I can but there seems no other explanation. And yet how can it be? How can he still be in the house and no one find him?'

'I don't know,' Sir Hugh responded shortly. 'All I do know is that your accursed twin has a great ability for landing on his feet! Even had he been taken I would have staked my blunt on his coming out all right, and since we know that he has not I'm as sure as I can be that he is well.'

Thoughtfully Rosamund sipped her sherry. 'But what are we to do about it?'

'I haven't yet decided. I could ride to Upavon in the morning, I suppose, though what good it would do I haven't the least notion.'

Rosamund shook her head despondently. 'What a tangle this all is, and how like Harry! He is so careless, you know, I would not be surprised if he had given us barely a thought! I only hope he does not do anything silly about that wretched ring!'

They were interrupted at that moment by the Duchess. She came into the room with a rustle of skirts and exclaimed, on seeing Sir Hugh: 'So you are back! No news, I suppose! What a naughty boy your brother is, my dear! I wonder you bother with him at all!' She accepted with a smile a glass of sherry and sank with a sigh onto the sofa. 'Do you have any notion of what to do now?' she inquired, looking from one to the other.

Sir Hugh shook his head. 'There seems little anyone can do, except wait, and hope he contrives to contact us.'

It was at this moment that a rider from Upavon arrived at the lodge and was admitted by the Duchess's gatekeeper. Unaware of the flurry into which his missive would cast the recipients he trotted sedately up the sweeping drive to dismount a few minutes late before the elegant mansion, and walked in a leisurely fashion to the large brass knocker.

13

'Well?' demanded Harry as the door opened softly.

Miss Davidson entered the room quietly and nodded. 'Yes, my lord, she's all tucked up nice and comfy, though I won't hesitate to tell you that I had some business to persuade her to lie down at all! But there, my bed is as comfy as you'd wish to meet, and she's young enough to go off in a minute.'

'Thank you. I'm very grateful. I would not want to upset her. Well, shall we get on?'

'Yes, my lord, if you are ready. The master's in his study right enough.'

'Good.' Impatiently Harry tossed back the covers with his good arm and swung his feet to the floor. As he did so a sudden feeling of dizziness threatened to overcome him, and he sank back onto the pillows. 'Damnation! Why do

I have to be so wretchedly weak?'

'Now, my lord, it's no more than you should have bargained for, and you four days in bed! You sit there for a moment while I fetch your clothes.'

Smiling, but obedient, Harry sat on the edge of the bed, his bad arm lying in a sling, watching as Miss Davidson shook out his shirt in a business-like fashion. 'I suppose it would not do to own to shyness,' he remarked as she turned back to him.

'Good gracious, my lord, what nonsense! Why should you be shy?'

'I'm a grown man, Davey,' he said, grinning at her.

'Grown indeed! You're little more than a lad!'

Harry grinned, and submitted meekly to her ministrations.

'I'm sure I think you're doing a wise thing,' said Miss Davidson, easing him carefully into the freshly laundered shirt. 'I'm not saying Miss Cressy would agree, for I know quite well she would not, besides being pretty cut up into the bargain. But you can't stay here, and that's a fact.'

'I know that well enough, Davey, and I'm glad you succeeded in persuading her out of the way.'

'That's as maybe, but I'll have you know, my lord, that I've had my eye on you. I've looked after Miss Cressy since her mother left us, and like a daughter she is to me, if I might be suffered to say so. What your intentions are I don't know, but that Miss Cressy is sweet on you is plain as a pike-staff! Well, I've not cared for the child all these years to see her cut up over some good-for-nothing Viscount, and even if the master doesn't send you for trial, which is a matter for him to decide, I don't want that lamb hurt, which she will be, if you don't take care!' She glared at him defiantly, her face flushed with emotion, and then returned to her task of dressing him.

Harry, who was both touched and amused by this speech, smiled at her, but said quite seriously: 'I don't think you need worry, Davey! My reputation might be quite sullied, but I am not so depraved, I believe, as to take advantage of a gently-bred young lady! If everything goes well for me, which, as you say, is far from decided, it would be a different matter. However, I shall not go into that now.'

Miss Davidson directed her searching gaze at him, and then nodded, apparently satisfied. Thereafter she dedicated herself to the task of dressing her patient. This was necessarily a slow process. Harry, although uncomplaining, found the whole business very painful, and was obliged several times to bite his lip as Miss Davidson inadvertently pulled the mending bone. At last it was done, however, and Harry, supporting himself with one hand against the wall, was as ready as he could be.

'There!' said Miss Davidson, giving his cravat a final twitch. 'Not what you're used to, I daresay, but we can't help that!'

'I'm sure it's far better than I could

manage,' Harry said, smiling down at her.

'You're a wicked one, and no mistake!' said Miss Davidson, reddening. 'I'm sure I should be glad if you were sent for trial!'

'Shame on you, Davey!' cried Harry, not deceived. 'I daresay you would cry as much as my poor sister.'

'Well, if you think that you're much mistaken,' she told him roundly. 'So much trouble as you've been I'll be glad to see you gone!'

Harry grinned. 'You deserve that I should kiss you for that!' he said, taking a purposeful step forward.

'You wouldn't dare!' she exclaimed, blushing and backing away.

He laughed. 'No, I shouldn't, indeed! I should be living in dread of your reprisals!'

'Get away with you,' she said in a scolding tone. 'If we're going downstairs let's be going! I haven't all day!'

'Very well,' said Harry meekly, his

eyes twinkling at her. 'But I fear I shall need some help. I can't trust my legs.'

Some minutes later Sir Joshua Kingman, seated at his desk before a pile of official papers, was surprised and irritated to be disturbed by a knock. He frowned in annoyance, having instructed his butler quite definitely that he should not be disturbed. Sighing, he called out sharply, and sat back to deliver a lecture. He was surprised almost immediately. Instead of the portly, balding figure he had expected he recognised the spare form of his daughter's maid, who peered round the door somewhat nervously.

'What is it, Miss Davidson?' he demanded irritably.

At that Miss Davidson opened the door wider, revealing to his astonished gaze a complete stranger, leaning heavily on Miss Davidson, his left arm in a sling.

'What the devil — ?' he ejaculated, starting out of his chair as the pair approached.

'Pray excuse the intrusion,' said Harry, bowing as low as he was able, 'Viscount Kearsley.' With a little difficulty he produced a card which he held out for Sir Joshua's inspection.

'I daresay,' said that bewildered gentleman, 'but in what way may I serve you? You need not stay, Miss Davidson.'

'On the contrary,' said the Viscount smoothly. 'What I have to say nearly concerns this good woman.'

'Concerns my daughter's abigail?' exclaimed Sir Joshua, becoming every minute more alarmed.

Carefully the Viscount shut the door. 'Sir Joshua,' he began, approaching the desk, 'you may remember, four days ago, that a villain of some sort was very nearly apprehended within your home, but, no doubt to the confusion of all concerned, vanished without trace.'

'Certainly I remember,' said Sir Joshua, eyeing his guest warily, 'but what has that to say to anything?'

Harry smiled ruefully. 'I happen to be he.'

Sir Joshua stared. 'What is this?' he demanded. 'If this is some sort of jest, my lord, I have to tell you that I do not find it amusing!'

Harry drew himself up a little taller. 'It is no joke, I assure you! I am he!'

'Indeed! Perhaps, sir, you would care to explain yourself, and also what this has to do with my daughter's abigail!'

'Certainly,' said Harry calmly, 'but are you sure you do not wish to call the gaoler?'

'My dear Viscount Kearsley, I am perfectly certain I am more than a match for you in your present condition, and I propose to summon no one until I learn how my daughter is involved!'

'Very well,' responded Harry with a twisted smile. 'The tale is simple enough. Your gaoler, an excellent fellow I make no doubt, inflicted a painful blow upon my shoulder, breaking the bone, I later discovered, and I managed to stagger into your daughter's apartments before I collapsed.'

'My daughter's apartments?' echoed the Justice, staring. 'But how can this be? I searched her rooms myself!'

'I know that,' responded Harry, a twinkle in his brown eyes. 'I was not to discover until much later just how close I came to being found!'

'Sir!' said Sir Joshua, controlling himself with a strong effort, 'I think you had better explain just what you are talking about!'

'Sir,' said Miss Davidson, stepping forward, 'if you will allow me I shall be happy to explain.'

'If you mean it is time for you to explain your part in this deplorable affair I entirely agree,' responded the magistrate coldly.

Undaunted by his quelling manner Miss Davidson nodded. 'As the Viscount says, he collapsed inside Miss Cressy's door. I didn't see it, but I came from the bedroom in time to see Miss Cressy jump up, in that impetuous way she has, and say I was to help to carry the poor man to her bed.'

Sir Joshua's eyes glinted, but all he said was: 'I see. Pray continue.'

'Well, needless to mention, I was horrified at first by the impropriety of it, a man, in such an innocent's bedroom, but she was quite determined, sir, and I could see that nothing would do but for me to help her. Besides, the poor man was quite unconscious and so pale I thought for a moment he was dead. That was when you came to the door, sir, wishful to see your daughter had come to no harm.' She looked at him anxiously for a moment, but as he said nothing she continued. 'And when, of course, she had persuaded you that no one had entered her room nothing would do but that I should nurse the poor young man back to health. It was obvious his shoulder was broken, and although I'm no expert, I set it well enough, I believe. I tried to persuade Miss Cressy to turn him over, but the sweet lamb would not hear of it, vowing she would sleep on the couch until he was mended. Which she did,' Miss Davidson added, not without pride. 'At first I was very worried about the Viscount, the wound being inflamed and his growing feverish. But he was right enough after a while, as you can see.'

Sir Joshua grunted, and eyed the patient from beneath his brows. 'I understand your disappearance well enough,' he said at last, 'and my daughter's part in the affair also, reprehensible though it may be. But perhaps, sir, you would care to explain your presence in my house at all!'

Harry was prepared for this. 'Of course,' he answered quickly. 'I came to recover some property of mine.'

The dark eyes snapped angrily. 'Explain yourself, young man!'

Several times during the ensuing tale did Sir Joshua glance grimly at the tall figure before him. Harry made no attempt to excuse himself, well aware that his dealings must seem both foolish and highly reprehensible in the eyes of this stiff-backed gentleman. Only in one instance was he less than truthful. All mention of his sister and her part in his affairs was studiously avoided, Harry calmly claiming all responsibility for his misdeeds.

Sir Joshua listened in silence. It went against the grain for him to admit it, even to himself, but he felt a strange admiration for the way the young man admitted his follies, with no attempt at excuse, all the time with his chin held high and his eyes steady. When he came to the story of the ring, however, Sir Joshua's brow puckered. 'There was no ring among the effects,' he said shortly, interrupting Harry's speech. 'Are you sure he had it on him?'

'Quite sure.'

Sir Joshua nodded and Harry continued. He had just reached the point where he was riding across to Upavon when the door flew open and Cressida ran into the room.

'Oh please, Papa,' she cried, grasping

his arm feverishly, 'do not listen to them! They do not know what they are saying!'

'Be quiet, child, this business does not concern you!'

'Papa, I will not be dismissed like that! It does concern me, very much! I shall not let you hang him!'

'Cressida!' said her father sternly. 'You will oblige me by leaving the room this instant and returning to your own apartment!'

To his astonishment she shook her head. 'No, Papa, I cannot. Do you think I can stand by while you commit poor Harry for trial? I cannot, Papa!'

Sir Joshua answered her gently. 'Child, you are over-wrought! This business is not your affair! You would do well to leave us!'

'I will not go!' Cressida cried, stamping one little foot.

'You are all of you quite foolish! Davey, I had thought you more trustworthy! Why did you let him do it?'

Miss Davidson met her reproachful eyes, and shook her head. Harry, with a glance at the magistrate, said soothingly: 'You would do better to leave us, Miss Kingman. There are matters you cannot understand!'

'Oh, you are as bad as all the rest!' she exclaimed, her voice breaking with emotion. 'It is you who do not understand! How can I stand by and see Papa get you hanged?'

'Cressida, I understand that you feel in some sense responsible for Kearsley, but — '

'Responsible?' she echoed, staring at him. 'I *love* him!'

This response stunned her auditors. No one, least of all Kearsley, had expected so open a declaration, and for a moment the three of them regarded her in embarrassed silence. Miss Davidson reacted first. She raised one hand to her eyes, brushing something away with a hasty gesture. Viscount Kearsley, who had not known until that moment how deep was his own affection, remained rooted to the spot, his face pale, and his eyes fixed upon Miss Kingman. At last Sir Joshua broke the silence.

'Cressida, you are overwrought,' he said calmly. 'You should rest for a while.'

She gave an unsteady laugh. 'Oh yes, it is easy for you to dismiss it, is it not? The only child, the little daughter with nothing to do but dream! Well, it is not so, Papa, and I tell you now, if you cause Harry to be hanged, or imprisoned, I shall never, never, forgive you.' Her voice was quiet, but there was nothing insincere about her speech. Her bosom rose and fell rapidly, and she fixed her father with a gaze so intent he had trouble in meeting it.

'You treat me unfairly, Cressida,' he said coldly. 'Do not you know that I must do my duty?'

'Your duty, Papa? What of your duty to me? Does my happiness mean nothing to you? How can you stand there and condemn Harry so calmly, knowing what you do must break my heart?'

Harry stepped forward now and turned her gently to face him. 'Cressida, look at me! Your father is right, you know. He must do as the law commands. You say you love me, but you are young, and will forget me quickly enough. Besides, I am an ill choice for you to champion.' He smiled wryly at her, but won no response.

'I daresay it might be so for you,' she said calmly, 'but if you think I shall forget you are mistaken. I know I am young and inexperienced and know little enough of the world, but I believed you when you told me you would change. You meant it, I know you did. So why should I not champion you? Papa will say I am too young to know my own mind, but indeed, Papa, I have aged ten years in the last three days! I *feel* it, can you not see it?'

Reluctantly he met those earnest blue eyes with his own troubled grey ones, and had to own the truth of it. And yet it was a hard decision to make. He loved his daughter as his own life, yet to see her married to a highwayman — He sighed, and transferred his gaze to the slim young man before him, his chin proudly raised and his eyes fixed steadily on the magistrate's face. He made an effort to speak.

'Sir, do you love my daughter?'

Harry looked at her as she turned her huge violet eyes anxiously to his face. 'Yes,' he answered simply, 'I believe I do.'

Cressida turned her now radiant countenance upon her father. 'Oh Papa, *now* do you see?'

He met that fervent gaze and smiled ruefully. 'Child, what am I to do with you? You are both of you so young, so feckless, however would you manage?'

Cressida wrinkled her brow. 'I don't know, Papa,' she replied honestly. 'I daresay it will be difficult at first for both of us, Harry particularly, but I know we would succeed because we want it so much.'

'And if I were to let you go, Kearsley, what about this ring?'

Harry shook his head. 'I have already decided not to pursue that matter any further, and bear his displeasure as best I might.'

Sir Joshua regarded him silently. He felt a curious liking for this strange, wild young man who had erupted so suddenly into his quietly ordered existence, and felt oddly inclined to let the children have their way. 'Very well,' he said at last, 'but there is one condition. The Earl must be made master of the whole, and should he disagree to your union, well, then I shall not be able to countenance it.'

Cressida, now that her point was won, stared at her father in amazement. 'You will do it?' she faltered anxiously, searching his face. 'You are not roasting me?'

He glanced down at her and gave her cheek a careless pinch. 'No, I am not roasting you, Cressida. I shall stand by my part, but I warn you, all may not yet be well with you. The Earl may take exception, you know, to the loss of an heirloom.'

'He might,' concurred Harry, 'but this heirloom is something different. It never was his, you see. It is passed to the grandson, and while I daresay he will be very annoyed it has disappeared, it is to my grandson I must explain myself.'

Sir Joshua's lips twitched. 'You do not care, do you, what he thinks of you.'

'No,' Harry agreed calmly. 'He already thinks me sadly racketty, you see. It will only confirm him in his opinion.'

'Oh Papa!' exclaimed Cressida, who had been silently brooding on her happiness. 'You are so good to me! Can you appreciate how *happy* you have made me?'

She looked adoringly up into his face and he smiled. 'Yes, child, I believe I can, but you will make a sadly ramshackle couple, you know.'

'Oh I know!' she cried, flinging her arms about his neck, 'but what does that matter? I am so happy!' She broke from him on the words, and, fumbling frantically for her handkerchief, ran from the room.

'That's women all over,' remarked Harry, watching her departure. 'Make 'em happy and they turn into waterin'-pots.'

Sir Joshua eyed him gravely. 'I own, Kearsley, that I am a little concerned about this business. I only hope you will find it in you to reform yourself.'

'I believe I may,' responded Harry frankly. 'Not to say it won't be difficult, because it will, dashed difficult, in fact, but I shall have all the help I need.'

Sir Joshua nodded thoughtfully. 'Well, I hope you may be right. I won't hide it from you, Kearsley, I had hoped to take Cressida to London myself next season, but since I can hardly turn up such an advantageous match I suppose I must be complacent.'

Harry was quick to catch the indulgent

twinkle in Sir Joshua's eye, and grinned in response. 'As to the London season, sir, I have an idea of my own as to that. My sister appears to be on the verge of making a very — er — advantageous match of her own, and I daresay will be happy to accommodate us!'

★ ★ ★

Harry's second letter arrived at Ashbourne on the following day. Rosamund, prepared this time, ran downstairs as soon as she heard the horse's hooves, and, having read the missive so rapidly that she understood barely one word in ten, sought out Sir Hugh and besought him distractedly to tell her what it was about as she was too much disturbed to read it. Sir Hugh obliged, taking the letter calmly from her agitated fingers, and telling her to sit quietly on the bench while he mastered the contents.

'Dear sister,' he read.

'You will be pleased to learn that since my last I have sorted things

318

wonderfully with Sir Joshua, who is to be so obliging as to forgive me my sins. Make haste to Upavon, dear Ros, for I desire more than anything to make you known to your future sister-in-law, an exquisite creature without whose help I should almost certainly have died.'

'Good heavens,' exclaimed Rosamund blankly.

'The doctor has visited me, and says Miss Davidson has made such excellent work of my shoulder that he apprehends no danger of my not regaining full use of the arm, so you see how indebted I am to this excellent household.

'The ring, unfortunately, seems not to be here, but I have resolved to search no more and to confess the whole to my father. I will tell you more when I see you.

'Yours in haste,

H.'

'Well!' exclaimed Rosamund, 'if only I had known he did not want that ring

I should never have taken it from that fellow!'

Sir Hugh smiled, but said: 'It is to be hoped he wants it back, for I cannot see what good a confession would do, besides worrying your father quite unnecessarily.'

'Oh dear,' said Rosamund worriedly, 'you are right, of course. I wonder if he will think it necessary? I do hope not! But tell me, do you think it is true about Harry being married?'

Sir Hugh scanned the letter again. 'I do not believe that even Harry would jest about such a thing.'

Rosamund looked thoughtfully at him. 'Neither do I. Oh dear, I only hope he is not marrying her out of gratitude!'

'My dear Rose!' exclaimed Sir Hugh laughing. 'Do you think your brother so hare-brained? No, I have every expectation of finding a jewel in Miss Kingman. I daresay she will suit him very well, and, with luck, will give him a run for his money!'

Rosamund chuckled. 'I do hope so!

How funny it is to think of Harry married! In fact, I don't think I shall believe it until he tells me himself!'

But when, a few hours later, she encountered her brother in the grounds of Upavon Manor where he and Cressida were walking, she sensed almost immediately that a change had come over her brother since he had been away. He was as cheerful and careless as ever but beneath this lay a reserve she had not previously encountered in him, and she realised that in a matter of days he had left behind his boyhood. It was only a matter of a minute, too, before she realised how good Cressida would be for him, regarding him worshipfully, yet not blindly, and depending implicitly upon his judgement. She sensed that it would be a successful marriage, each partner deriving benefit from the match, and was secretly thankful that Harry's wild career should have been brought to so natural a close. If she felt a little saddened that they must now draw apart it was only something she had seen approaching for some months, and was in a way glad that it was Harry who had made the break.

Even if she had found Cressida designing and wilful she must have loved her, but when she drew her a little away from Harry and Hugh she soon discovered that there was much to love in her youth and determination. She felt that her brother would have been hard put to find a better bride, and any doubts she had felt over the suddenness of the engagement she allowed to disappear.

'I don't think you need worry about them,' said Hugh, watching as the two girls wandered into the orchard.

Harry smiled. 'I was a little, I must admit. We've been so close, she and I, I thought she might not quite like it at first.'

'It had to come, however. One of you was bound to marry.'

'Yes,' said Harry, casting the baronet a sly look, 'but I own, I had half expected it to be Rosamund.'

Sir Hugh met the look blandly. 'Naturally she will marry before too long. It's just a question of time.'

'I rather thought,' said Harry carelessly, 'that you and she might make a match of it.'

'You did, did you? I can't imagine why!'

'Oh, I daresay it was just something I noticed. She can't keep things from me, can't Ros, and I think I know you well enough, sir, to tell when you've a decided preference for someone's company.'

'And you, sir,' declared Hugh, 'are a scoundrel! Did you think to urge me on?'

'Well,' replied Harry frankly, 'I did think you might need a little push, yes. You've been making such damned heavy work of it!'

'Thank you!' exclaimed Sir Hugh, eyeing him frostily. 'When I need a push from you, Kearsley, I shall ask for it!'

Harry grinned. 'But naturally you will, sir! I never doubted you for a moment!'

Sir Hugh cast him a fulminating glance, and then turned on his heel and marched back to the house. Harry, having watched him for a moment, chuckled softly to himself, and went in search of his sister.

He found her in the orchard apparently engaged in the discussion of some weighty subject with his betrothed. He hesitated for a moment but then Rosamund turned and smiled at him.

'Well,' he said cheerfully, 'you need worry no longer, dearest sister. I have given your reluctant swain such a shove in the back you will not have the mortification of seeing me married much before you!'

Both ladies gasped and Rosamund looked at him horrified for a moment before exclaiming: 'Harry! Whatever have you been saying?'

'Oh, nothing very much,' he replied carelessly, his eyes twinkling at her, 'but I did think he needed a little encouragement to be brought up to scratch, you know, and who better to do it than I?'

'No one,' replied his sister hotly. 'Oh, whatever must he think? Harry, how could you?'

'Very easily, my dear. A word was all it took, though I must admit he didn't seem as diverted by it as I'd expected.'

'Diverted?' echoed his harassed twin hollowly. 'Harry, don't you know that above all things Sir Hugh despises match-makers? He has been pursued for so long, too! Oh, he must think me quite odious!'

'I don't see why,' said Harry, giving the problem his consideration. 'After all, it's as plain as a pikestaff he's nutty about you, and even if he is at his last prayers I don't see that it signifies very much.'

'You're just saying that to goad me!' replied his sister, eyeing him with dislike. 'You know very well Sir Hugh is one of the kindest, most generous men we have ever met, and as for being in his dotage — '

'Oh lord!' exclaimed Harry, revolted. 'Don't plague me with tales of his goodness, I beg of you, or I shall think I've served you a very back-handed turn! Sir Hugh is a trump, I agree, but if you're going to talk such fustian about his generosity I shall wash my hands of you!'

'Well, isn't he generous?' Rosamund demanded. 'Hasn't he dedicated himself to solving our problems like no one else would dream of doing?'

'Naturally he has, but don't try to tell me it was pure altruism, my love, because it don't wash!' Harry told her frankly. 'Are you seriously telling me you don't know he's been trying to fix his interest all these weeks?'

'Yes! No. Oh Harry, don't goad me, please! I need time to think. Why, I don't even know that I want to be married!'

'Well!' exclaimed Harry disgustedly.

'Of all the plumpers! Do you think I'm blind? You can't go around smelling of April and May for weeks on end without someone noticing! Besides,' he added honestly, 'if you don't marry him I shall be hard put to know how I'm going to introduce Cressy to the ton!'

'Harry!' exclaimed the horrified young ladies.

'Oh Harry!' said Cressida, shocked. 'How can you say such dreadful things? As if I minded about going to London!'

'Well if you don't I do,' replied her betrothed frankly. 'You deserve some pleasure before you settle down to a lifetime with me, after all, and if Ros ain't Lady Eavleigh I'm dashed if I can see how it is to be contrived!'

'You'll forgive me if I don't take quite the same view,' said Rosamund acidly. 'As for smelling like April and May, as you call it, I can't imagine what gave you such an idea!'

Harry smiled down at her affectionately. 'You forget, sweet Ros, how well I know you! Did you think I'd mind? I don't, I promise you. I admit, when I met Sir Hugh first he seemed quite an antique, but I meant it when I said he was a trump. He is, Ros, you know, and will suit you admirably. Why can't you admit what you feel?'

Rosamund shrugged. 'Because I've been frightened, I suppose, that he didn't feel for me — in that way. It wouldn't surprise me, you know, if he didn't, especially when Papa invited him down for just that reason.'

'Well, if you ask me, Ros,' said Harry candidly, 'if you don't take care you're going to have him posting off to London before too long! There's nothing to hold him now, after all!'

It seemed as though Harry's words were justified. Wandering back to the house they were greeted by the intelligence that Sir Hugh had departed, having stayed only to take his leave of his host before setting out for Ashbourne, with the intention, he said, of departing thence for London.

14

It was with an effort that Rosamund forced herself not to think about Hugh. She was a little hurt that he had chosen to go off without even saying his goodbyes, but when she came to think of how Harry had treated him, well, she really could not be surprised. There was only one reason that she could think of why Sir Hugh should have chosen to remain any longer, and the necessary reflection did little for her peace of mind. She endeavoured, therefore, to put him from her mind, spending almost all her time with Harry and Cressida, or at Ashbourne with the Duchess. Very often she succeeded very well, for she was fond of Harry, and found the Duchess excellent company. More frequently than she would have liked, however, she found her thoughts dwelling on the adventures the three of them had had, and often caught herself up in wishing that he had been there to partake of some joke. It was all too provoking! Barely a month before she would have been overjoyed had Sir Hugh decided not to enter her life, and to think that in such a short space of time she could discover her peace to be centred wholly on one nearly twice her age! It was with a little shock that she realised just how long her dependence had been on Sir Hugh. She had been relying on him for far longer than she had realised, and when she considered how they had both imposed upon him she could only think it remarkable that he had not left them sooner. It was a lowering thought that she who had always prided herself on her self-reliance should be so dependent on another being for her comfort. And then she thought how reassuring it had been to have someone as steady as Hugh at her side, someone who would not, like Harry, rush off on some start, but had proved as ready even as Harry to embark on the most outrageous of exploits. As she thought of this her brow puckered. Really, it was most extraordinary! That Sir Hugh, who had been content for so many years to lead a comfortable and cushioned existence, should suddenly be plummeted into the midst of adventure and far from being shocked had shown himself to be a valuable member of the company was really quite extraordinary. How odd that she had not considered that before! Sir Hugh was, by repute, one of the staidest, most steady men of society, and yet instead of quailing at the very mention of a confrontation with the military he had plunged into the affray with very little thought for the consequences. When she thought of this Rosamund knew a little guilt. They had embroiled him in their affairs with very little consideration for his wishes, but the extraordinary thing was, and the more she thought about it the more certain it seemed, he had enjoyed it all.

Rosamund sighed, and pushed away

the embroidery on which she had been trying to concentrate. Harry had that day visited their father, and the matter of the engagement had been broached. He was surprised, naturally, and at first seemed inclined to dismiss the whole business. The gentle insistence of his son, however, had served to convince him, and he had agreed to pay a visit to Upavon on the following day. All this Rosamund had discovered earlier that evening, and the information that Harry had brought, that her father wished for her return, had cast a cloud over her existence. Daviot, with Harry gone, would be very dull, and there seemed no possibility of relief. Of course she would retain the friendship of the Duchess, but a distance of seventeen miles was too far for a daily visit, and it seemed likely that her life would fall into dull and boring routine.

She set out for Daviot three days later. The Duchess, conscious of her father's claims, had made no attempt to detain her longer, but had extracted from her a faithful promise that she would write to let her new friend know how she was going on. It seemed very strange to be returning to Daviot alone. Shut up in the Duchess's elegant travelling carriage she could not but reflect on the last occasion of her travelling in it, when she and Hugh had recovered Harry's ring. How long ago it all seemed, to be sure! Now, as she sat in the corner gently swaying with the movement of the chaise, she could almost believe it had happened to someone else.

Her thoughts were interrupted. As with another traveller, there were suddenly sounds of confusion from in front, and the coach gave a sudden lurch that resulted in her being cast onto the floor. Shaken, but unhurt, she picked herself up and realised that the carriage had come to a standstill. Mechanically dusting her skirts she let down the window and leant out to see what was the trouble.

An extraordinary sight met her

eyes. In the middle of the road was a masked man astride a large chestnut. He was very broad, and the battered tricorn rammed down hard onto his head created a highly disreputable appearance. Interestedly Rosamund noticed that he held the reins in his teeth, keeping the coachman covered with two heavy plain pistols. She found herself thinking that it was really a good idea, and then caught herself up as the rider approached the chaise. He was certainly very big; indeed, she could not remember when she had last seen such a large man. His eyes glinted dangerously at her as he gained the doorway, and then, to her surprise, uttered something unintelligible. She stared at him in amazement, and then, as she realised the reason for his peculiar speech a stifled giggle escaped her. The highwayman looked taken aback, and then, with what Rosamund thought was a sheepish look, he thrust one of his pistols into his pocket and removed the reins from his mouth.

'The gewgaws!' he demanded, very roughly, waving his remaining pistol in a threatening manner.

'I haven't any,' responded Rosamund calmly.

Again the highwayman stared at her. 'The gewgaws!' he repeated after a moment with a little less conviction.

Rosamund shook her head. To her surprise, however, the highwayman did not seem daunted, in fact she had the strangest feeling that he was smiling at her. And then she knew. With a gasp she clapped her hand to her mouth and sat back suddenly onto the padded seat.

'Now, Miss,' growled the highwayman, awfully, 'be you'm goin' to gimme them gewgaws or not?'

'Oh, don't shoot, don't shoot!' she cried, causing the coachman on his box to shake his head wretchedly. 'You can have anything you want!'

'Ha! That I can!' said Hugh, wrenching open the door with his free hand. 'An' I've a mind for you, my pretty!'

'Oh!' wailed Rosamund, lifting her skirts to prevent them getting dirty as she descended to the road. 'What do you want with me?'

'Ha!' growled the man, extending his hand to assist her onto the horse.

It was with horror that the groom and coachman realised the rogue had their passenger seated sideways before him on his horse. The coachman gave a gasp and seemed about to jump down from his box, but at that moment his colleague gave an exclamation and pointed dumbly at the highwayman. He was backing away slowly, and the pistol, pressed firmly against the lady's temple, showed plainly that he would have no scruples about shooting her.

'Lay any information and the lady's dead!' the fellow proclaimed roughly. 'Turn about and gettee home!'

The coachman hesitated, but Rosamund, who was enjoying herself hugely, cried out: 'Oh please, please do as he says! I'm so frightened! Go back to Ashbourne, please, before he kills us all!'

This seemed to be pretty sound advice. With one more glance at the pair on the horse the coachman gathered the reins and began turning his vehicle. In a moment the carriage was facing the other direction, and then, with an exhortation from Rosamund that he would not consider her, the coachman whipped up his team and set off down the road.

For a moment the two were silent, watching as the dust gradually settled back onto the road. And then Rosamund laughed.

'Hugh, you idiot!' she exclaimed. 'Whatever are you playing at?'

He grinned and pulled off his hat. 'I thought you would appreciate it,' he said, loosening the strings of his mask. 'It seemed most appropriate.' He tossed the mask away, and smiled down at her in a way that made Rosamund's heart beat very fast.

'We ought to get down,' she said, a little breathlessly, lowering her eyes. 'Your horse won't enjoy this for much longer!'

Recollecting himself Sir Hugh jumped down and turned to lift Rosamund from the saddle.

'What are we going to do now?' she asked, looking up at him expectantly.

He smiled at her. 'I have my curricle in the bushes over there, a more suitable conveyance, I believe, than a single horse.'

She laughed. 'Yes indeed! Will you convey me to Daviot, please, now that you have sent away my chaise?'

Sir Hugh gave her a funny smile. 'I would dearly love to, but I'm afraid we have a lot of travelling to do.'

'Travelling?' she echoed, looking up at him sharply.

'We're going to London,' he said casually, catching the horse's reins and preparing to lead him away.

'To London?' she repeated stupidly, feeling that she had somehow failed to understand him.

He nodded. 'I think it wisest, don't you? Of course, we could go to Gloucestershire, but I think you will find London far more to your taste.'

Rosamund felt a peculiar sinking sensation in the pit of her stomach. 'Sir Hugh,' she began, forcing her voice to be steady, 'what are you planning?'

He turned now and smiled at her, a warm, affectionate smile, and one which under different circumstances she would have been overjoyed to see. 'We are eloping,' he responded, as though it was the most natural thing in the world.

Reluctantly Rosamund laughed. 'Oh you are ridiculous,' she said, feeling slightly relieved. 'What are you really planning?'

'I am really planning an elopement,' he replied, taking her arm and persuading her on.

'But this is madness!' she exclaimed, staring up at him. 'You do not know what you are saying!'

He stopped now and turned her to face him. 'I know only too well,' he replied gently. 'In fact, I am only doing what I should have done a week ago!'

To her annoyance Rosamund felt tears pricking her eyes.

'Please, you don't know what you are doing! It is all because of what Harry — '

'Pardon me, but it is nothing to do with Harry. I love you and I want you to marry me. But naturally if you don't want to elope with me we shall not, although I can't help feeling that the staff in Grosvenor Square will be a little disappointed if they don't get a mistress after all.'

She gave an unsteady laugh. 'Hugh, I wish you would be sensible! How can I elope with you? Why, I have nothing ready!'

'As a matter of fact everything you need is in London already. I saw your father two days ago and conveyed your clothes and your maid to London myself. But naturally, if you do not want to marry me then I shall convey them back again.'

'You've seen Papa?' echoed Rosamund, ignoring the latter part of his speech. 'Oh, what did he say?'

Hugh smiled. 'He was delighted. In fact, he was so very glad I had decided to marry you that he was even prepared to overlook the unconventional manner of our wedding. To tell the truth, my dear, I think your dear father finds you a bit of a handful, and then, you know, there was that unfortunate business about that other elopement, and he was swiftly brought to see that the sooner you are married the better it will be for all of us!'

'Oh!' exclaimed Rosamund, her eyes flashing at him. 'How odious you are! Am I to have no shred of reputation left?'

'None at all, my dear, unless you marry me. But I do think we ought to hurry. I have a special licence, you know, in my pocket, so there is really no reason for us to delay.'

Of a sudden Rosamund felt absurdly shy. She was unable to meet his gaze and stood staring at his greatcoat, nervously twisting her fingers.

'Rosamund,' said Sir Hugh sharply. 'Rosamund, look at me.'

She did now as she was bid, meekly meeting his eyes.

'Rosamund, will you marry me?'

She hesitated, reading in his eyes the love she felt in her own heart. 'Hugh, are you sure?'

'Of course I am! Do you think I should have gone to all this trouble if I weren't?'

She giggled weakly at that and said: 'No, I suppose you wouldn't.'

'Then will you marry me?'

'You must be mad, Hugh, to want to marry me!'

He assented readily, and Rosamund, finding one strong arm around her waist and a hand tilting up her face, decided that he had best be humoured.

Other titles in the
Linford Romance Library

SAVAGE PARADISE
Sheila Belshaw

For four years, Diana Hamilton had dreamed of returning to Luangwa Valley in Zambia. Now she was back — and, after a close encounter with a rhino — was receiving a lecture from a tall, khaki-clad man on the dangers of going into the bush alone!

PAST BETRAYALS
Giulia Gray

As soon as Jon realized that Julia had fallen in love with him, he broke off their relationship and returned to work in the Middle East. When Jon's best friend, Danny, proposed a marriage of friendship, Julia accepted. Then Jon returned and Julia discovered her love for him remained unchanged.

NEATH PORT TALBOT LIBRARY
AND INFORMATION SERVICES

1	9/10	25		49		73	
2		26		50		74	
3		27		51		75	
4		28		52		76	
5		29		53		77	
6		30		54		78	
7		31		55		79	
8		32		56		80	
9		33		57		81	
10		34		58		82	
11		35		59		83	
12		36		60		84	
13		37		61		85	
14		38		62		86	
15		39		63		87	
16		40		64	12/22	88	
17		41		65		89	
18		42		66		90	
19		43		67		91	
20		44		68	3/6	92	
21		45		69		COMMUNITY SERVICES	
22		46		70			
23		47		71		NPT/111	
24		48		72			